D1226638

Weekly Reader Children's Book Club presents

LONE SEAL PUP

ARTHUR CATHERALL

LONE SEAL PUP

Illustrated by John Kaufmann

New York: *E. P. DUTTON & CO., INC.*

First published in the U.S.A. 1965 by E. P. Dutton & Co., Inc. •

Printed in the U.S.A. •

Library of Congress catalog card number: 65-21274 •

Weekly Reader Children's Book Club Edition

Contents

1	An Ice-Baby is Born	11
2	The Ice Breaks Up	22
3	A Walrus Warrior	32
4	A Cry for Help	45
5	Ah-Leek the Lonely	54
6	Battle Royal	64
7	Guardians of the Beach	71
8	Caught between Two Fires	82
9	Prisoner on the Beach	89
10	The Sea Claims a 'Good Spirit'	104

1

An Ice-Baby is Born

WHEN the screaming wind dropped, the silence which followed was so great that it seemed as if the world of snow and ice held no life at all. For eight months the sea had been completely frozen over, so that it was difficult to tell where frozen salt water ended and the snow-covered land of northern Alaska began.

With spring on the way and the sun shining pale yellow from low down on the horizon, the glare from the frozen landscape could blind a man in a few hours if he did not protect his sight. Yet ice glare went almost unnoticed by the animal moving slowly along the fringe of sea and land. His wet black nose and his small ears served him far better than eyes, for scents and sounds carried far.

Gaunt from a winter of semi-starvation, the big polar bear was hard to see, for his thick, cream-coloured fur blended so well with the snow and ice that when he stopped moving he became almost invisible. He had stopped when the first faint sound came, and his small triangular-shaped head was swinging on his long snaky neck as he sniffed the faintest of breezes blowing from the sea. He was very hungry indeed.

Then the silence was broken again. From far across the ice came a thin baby wail. It was such a tiny cry that no man would have heard it, but the polar bear did, and he knew what kind of animal it came from. At this time of the year the young seals were being born, and that piping cry was made by a seal which was only a few hours old.

The bear swung his head in the direction of the sound; his black nose twitched hungrily as he tried to catch the scent of seal. Then with his big padded feet making no more than a slurred whisper he started out across the frozen sea. Food he must have, and he knew that seals were forced to come up through their breathing-holes in the ice. Baby seals had to be brought to the air more often than their mothers, so there was more hope of a meal now than there had been for some time.

His eyes saw nothing but snow-covered ice, but his nose soon told him that he was moving in the right direction. Here and there the seals, who lived under the ice during the dark storm-ridden months of winter, kept breathing-holes open. When they badly needed a rest they would break the thin film of ice which covered the holes and come up to flop about for a few minutes on the surface.

The polar bear found a seal-hole, and there was a smell of seal in the air. What was more, the water in the three-foot-deep breathing-hole was only starring over with new ice. The bear licked his lips. A seal *was* using this hole and, if it was a mother seal, with a new-born baby, she would come up for air again very soon.

Backing away from the darkness of the breathing-hole the bear lay down to wait. He had to be far enough away from the hole for the seal not to recognize him as an enemy. He had to be near enough to be able to rush forward and make his kill before the seal could drop back into the water. He chose his position so that the faint breeze was blowing over the hole towards him. It would bring the scent of the seal to him, but his own scent would be blown away. Now it was a question of waiting.

He had not made a mistake, for below the ice there was a mother seal with her new-born baby, Ah-Leek. It was this baby's cry which had warned the bear that he might get a meal if he was quick and quiet. The mother had lived under the ice throughout the winter. The bitter cold did not worry her, and there was no shortage of food, for fish were plentiful.

Like all seals, Ah-Leek's mother had several breathing-holes which she kept open. Visiting them in turn, she would thrust up her head, jabbing at the ice with her nose. Then, after she had made a small hole, she would nibble at the edges of the ice until she had broken it all away. Sometimes she would climb up on to the ice above, and rest under the brilliant stars, or in a white world lit by the pink, green and oddly luminous white of the northern lights.

Now, unaware that there was an enemy lying on the ice above, she was getting ready to climb out on to the ice for a rest. Her baby had been born no more than an hour. She had licked his fuzzy white fur from the ends of his dainty little back flippers to the top of his round head.

She had given him his first feed, and now she heaved him out of the water on to a narrow ledge in the ice of her breathing-hole. The breathing-hole was like the manholes seen in city streets, except that it was of ice. Three feet down from the upper world there was water—freezingly cold water; though that did not worry either the mother or her baby.

She bobbed up against the thin film of ice already forming over the water in the hole, and as the ice broke it produced a thin tinkling sound, almost musical in the awful stillness of this frozen world.

It was only a tiny sound, but it told the polar bear that something was happening. He inched forward a little, and made sure he could get a good grip on the ice with his back paws. Then he carefully covered his black nose with one of his forepaws. Lying thus, he might easily have been mistaken for just another little mound of frozen snow.

Ah-Leek's mother broke all the ice in the hole, and looked up at the sky. She could not see the sun, but the sky was cloudless just now and intensely blue. Gathering herself for the effort she gave a mighty kick with her rear flippers and shot up out of the water as if she had been propelled by a catapult.

She did not attempt to get out on the ice yet. She knew very well the dangers there were in the world above. Even in winter some of her friends had gone up on to the ice and not come back. Polar bears spent their time going from breathing-hole to breathing-hole, and in addition there were other enemies. If the Eskimoes who lived in this barren world ran short of meat they came down to the sea.

Like the polar bears, they were prepared to squat motionless by the side of a breathing-hole, waiting for some unlucky seal to come out for a rest. Life could be dangerous even in the blackness of winter. Now that the sun had returned to the arctic it was even more dangerous.

Ah-Leek's mother shot out of the water, high enough for her head and shoulders to bob up above the surface of the ice. She was able to have a quick look round before she splashed back in the water. Her eyes were big and brown but, like the eyes of most other animals, they were better at seeing enemies which moved. She must have seen the silent mound of fur and muscle, but the polar bear did not look like an enemy.

Three times she bobbed up, and each time looked in a different direction. It was a trick passed on to her by her mother; but it was also a trick the polar bear knew. He lay flat, his tell-tale black nose-tip hidden behind a paw, but he was watching with half-open eyes. The scent of the seal maddened him, for he was starving, but he kept perfectly still.

In this land, where food was so scarce for the hunter, patience and cleverness were necessary, and the bear knew how quick a seal could be. And a mother seal with a new-born baby was always more cautious than ordinary seals. If he kept still for a few minutes he might have a good meal.

It seems as if the mother seal would never be satisfied as she bobbed up then dropped back into the water. The bear was beginning to think she must have seen him, and was nerving himself for a lightning rush forward, hoping to catch her as she bobbed up. But it was not necessary. Ah-Leek's mother finally decided it was safe to leave the water. She gave her son a last reassuring lick, then with a powerful flick of her tail flippers shot upwards again. This time, however, she hooked her fore flippers over the edge of the hole and hung there.

She had not been out on the ice for almost two weeks, and the world seemed a vastly different place. The sun was shining and, because a recent storm had blown most of the powdery snow into wave-like ripples, the uncovered ice looked blue and green in places.

Not looking for beauty, Ah-Leek's mother stared around

the whole horizon, and nothing moved. No bird swept through the air, though they would be coming soon; no animal walked. There were no black dots to suggest other seals were out on the ice; but she was so anxious to stretch, and relax, that she decided it was safe.

The polar bear, because he was so perfectly still, and had hidden his black nose, looked to her like a small mound of ice. She gave a little hitch and heaved herself so high out of the hole that she was on the point of toppling forward on to the ice itself when Ah-Leek wailed.

It was only the third time he had wailed since being born almost an hour earlier. He had drunk deep of his mother's milk, closed his eyes and gone to sleep. He had been asleep while she licked him from his tiny hind flippers to the top of his fuzzy furred head. Now he woke, and he wanted his mother. He gave a thin, plaintive wail, and it made all the difference to what was going to happen.

His mother half turned to look down the breathing-hole. As she did so the polar bear heaved himself up. He was trembling in his eagerness. Three times in the past five days he had been at a seal-hole, and missed a meal by a fraction of a second. He did not mean to be disappointed a fourth time.

As he lifted himself up, and shot forward with amazing quickness for such a large animal, Ah-Leek cried for a fourth time. His mother, suddenly anxious, heaved herself backwards off the rim of the hole and began to fall towards the water just as the polar bear swung his powerful right paw.

The mother seal missed death by no more than an inch, and felt the wind as the massive paw swept just above her head. A second later there was a splash from below, and the bear, who slithered forward so quickly that he almost fell into the hole, jerked his head back as water spouted up and into his eyes.

With a terrifying growl of rage he dabbed a paw downwards, though he knew from past experience that he would not be able to reach his intended meal. The seal, even as it vanished below the surface, had shot a quick glance upwards and seen the triangular head, the bared teeth and the flashing eyes.

Her first thought was to swim deep down and far away from the hole. Then she remembered her new baby. She turned in the water quicker than thought, and surfaced. Ah-Leek was still on the ledge, and again he wailed. Had he kept silent the danger would have been past within a minute, for the bear was wise enough to know he could never catch a seal once it had got into the safety of the breathing-hole.

It was Ah-Leek's baby cry which brought the bear back to the hole. He stood with his great forepaws on the ice-rim and looked down. He could vaguely make out the shadowy form of the mother seal as she kept just below the surface of the water. Yet the scent of seal, warm and tantalizing, came up strongly to him.

Ah-Leek, growing impatient for more milk, wailed again, and this time even the short-sighted eyes of the polar bear made out the tiny figure curled up under the ledge, no more than three feet below the surface of the ice.

The polar bear dabbed a forepaw tentatively down the hole, then, realizing he could never reach the seal pup that way, he lay full length on the ice, and reached down, sweeping his paw clumsily from side to side.

Less than an hour old, and not yet afraid of anything, Ah-Leek began to move towards the paw. He thought that anything which moved must be his mother, and he was already hungry again.

If the bear had possessed fingers instead of blunt claws he could have lifted the young seal out quite easily. One claw did hook into Ah-Leek's fuzzy mass of white hair, and dragged the young seal almost to the lip of the ice-ledge. Then the claw broke free.

Knowing that he had touched the seal, but unable to see what he was doing, the bear drew his forepaw out so that he could look down into the hole. He was lying half across the hole and cutting off the daylight. Ah-Leek, wanting his mother, wailed again—the impatient wail of a hungry baby. The cry excited the bear even more, and down came his left forepaw, the blunt claws scooping for his victim.

In that instant something black and shiny came up out of the water. Ah-Leek's mother was terrified. Even the distant scent of a polar bear frightened her; but, when she saw that huge paw come down, fear for her baby made her do something desperately brave. She shot upwards, broke the surface of the water, and with one quick movement scooped Ah-Leek off his icy shelf.

She rose so quickly that she struck the bear's paw with the top of her head. He felt the touch, and scooped quick as lightning. For the second time in minutes the mother seal was within touching distance of death—and escaped.

There was a splash, and the hungry polar bear heaved himself upwards the better to see what had happened. He knew even before he looked that he had lost. The water below was agitated, but there was no sign of a seal. With a disappointed growl he licked the salt water from his nose and jowl. His hunger seemed even worse now.

For a few moments he stood staring down into the hole, then turned away to look round the ice-field. He knew the seal would have to come up for air, and more quickly than usual, because she had a baby with her. If he could get to the next breathing-hole before her, then his luck might change. He sniffed and got a scent.

Down below, Ah-Leek was being rushed at express speed through the icy waters. It was a strange world, this sea below the ice. For the first time for months it was being lit up by light seeping through the six-foot-thick ceiling of ice, and the light was drawing all kinds of living creatures upwards. Fish which had lived happily far below during the darkness of the winter were now moving about in schools just below the ice.

During the winter a coating of green, brown and even pink had come to life on the underside of the ice. The coloured vegetation contained food on which fish, shrimps, lugworms, and even a few starfish were nibbling. Ah-Leek's mother was hungry, for she had eaten nothing for more than a day, and she could have caught a handsome meal with the minimum of trouble just then.

She was not thinking of food. She could hold her breath for a long time, but baby seals have to learn to hold their breath, just as they have to learn to swim. Nature had made the seal pup pinch his nostrils tight and close his mouth the moment water closed over his head; but now his heart was struggling, and his mother could feel the fluttering beat of it. He must have air, or die.

Like a dark torpedo she raced through the water towards the nearest breathing-hole, scattering a school of tom-cod who thought she was after one of them. She saw the hole ahead, recognizing it by the stronger light shining down on to the water. Then as she got near she saw that two other seals were waiting with their babies. There was at least one other seal in the hole—and no room for her and Ah-Leek. No room, and the next hole was almost a hundred yards away!

2

The Ice Breaks Up

AH-LEEK's mother never hesitated. Normally she was quite a timid creature, but with her baby's life hanging by a thread she rushed towards the hole and bustled the two other mothers to one side. Like a black phantom she swept up into the air, jostling two other seals which were breathing there, and a moment later Ah-Leek was pushed up into the hole.

He gave a weak little sigh, and after two or three deep breaths the feeble fluttering of his heart-beat changed. It grew stronger even as his mother bared her teeth at the two strangers in the water alongside.

She kept Ah-Leek's head in the air for another minute or so, then sank down with him and rushed back to the breathing-hole where he had been born. She felt sure no other seal would go there for some time, since it now carried with it a strong smell of polar bear.

From then on she was like an anxious sentry, pushing Ah-Leek on to the ice shelf only when she was forced to leave him to seek food for herself. He lived on his mother's milk, which was like rich cream, and grew plumper in amazing fashion. Yet he never ceased his wailing for food. The only time he was quiet was when he was asleep, or when, after he was two weeks old, his mother took him out on to the ice to show him the world above.

With his fuzzy coat already beginning to look a little tattered, he lay on the ice and gazed about with his big brown eyes at the strange whiteness. It was a world which had changed considerably even in the short time he had been alive. Now it was no longer silent or deserted.

The sun was mounting higher in the heavens every day, and staying longer above the horizon. On shore the snow and ice were melting, and to the beaches were coming tens of thousands of birds. Some of them, the terns, had made a journey of many thousands of miles from the distant antarctic. Here they had been born, and here the mother birds would lay their eggs and hatch their young.

Wild geese began to appear overhead, flying in beautiful V-formations. They made the air ring with their triumphant bugling. White swans came, and sandhill cranes. Eider ducks arrived, and wherever they bobbed and preened there was a continuous murmur from them of 'A-uh . . . a-uuuh . . . a-uh . . . a-uuh'.

Flocks of snipe and sandpipers arrived, and snow buntings looking more like snowflakes than birds as the sun lit up their wings. In addition to all these were the gulls, and some of them were pirates. They patrolled up and down the coastline looking for birds who had caught fish. Others kept up a constant watch over the areas where the snow was melting and birds were already busy with their egg-laying. Woe betide any mother who left her nest for even a few minutes! The chances were that when she came back there would be nothing more than broken eggshells left.

The sun was growing warmer every day, and the ice was beginning to break up. There were stretches of open water, and when a strong wind began to blow the whole mass of ice started to drift away from the shore. For the first time for many months waves creamed up on the beaches again.

Ah-Leek hardly knew anything of this. Like all baby seals his one thought was of food, and that meant his mother. She was still providing him with an abundance of cream-like milk. He hardly ever seemed satisfied, yet he grew bigger and fatter. Whenever she left him to seek food for herself he cried like a heartbroken child.

Nor was he the only one. The winter silence was a thing of the past, for all over the ice-field seal pups were wailing as they called for their mothers; then quite suddenly their cries began to grow louder and sound even more heartbroken. An extraordinary thing was happening. It was something they could not understand, and it happened to Ah-Leek as well.

His mother seemed to be losing her love for him. Though he wailed for her she began to stray from him more and more, and for longer periods. The ice had now broken up completely into countless thousands of small floes and ice-pans. Ah-Leek had been taught to swim, and had grown to like sitting out on the ice, basking in the sun.

Then, one terrible day, his mother vanished. Several times

he had seen her playing with other full-grown seals. They seemed strangely excited and at times swept through the water at speeds far greater than Ah-Leek could manage.

When his mother returned to him after these exciting chases she would feed him and then carefully comb his fur with her fore flippers. By now the young seal was beginning to look less of a cuddly baby. His fuzzy white hair was coming off each time his mother combed him. Now he was more yellow and brown than white. The day when Ah-Leek became an orphan his mother gave him a last careful combing, then they both dived into the sea.

This was a game they had played a number of times, though the young seal was now growing tired of it. His mother swam one way round the ice-pan, Ah-Leek swam round the other way. They met, touched noses, then each swam back, to meet on the side where they had dived into the water.

Ah-Leek swam round the ice-floe, but his mother seemed to be slower than usual. He kept swimming until he was back where he started and did not see her. Then, because Ah-Leek was rather spoiled, as most seal pups are, he gave a plaintive wail and stopped swimming. His head looked like a shiny yellow ball as he bobbed gently up and down, waiting and wailing.

After a minute or so, as his mother did not appear, he wailed even louder. Then, sudden fear making his little brow pucker into a frown of worry, he began to swim as quickly as he could round the floe. He went the whole way round, and still there was no sign of his mother.

Hastily he heaved himself on to the edge of the ice and waddled all over the floe. Now he was crying out in anger for his mother. He was sure she was playing a game with him. When she still did not appear he flopped back into the sea again, and swam round the floe several times, sure that she was only playing.

All over the broken-up ice-field seal pups were crying louder than they had ever cried before. Quite suddenly they had all been deserted. They were bulging with fat, and were in no danger of starving. All of them had been taught to swim. All had watched mothers dart like dark javelins into schools of tom-cod, to single out one particular fish and chase him until the prize had been won. Yet there was scarcely a seal pup in those icy waters who had caught a fish for himself. They had seen how it was done, but had been too well fed and comfortable to bother trying for themselves.

Now, though they hardly realized it, they had been left to fend for themselves. They must learn to hunt for their own food, or starve. The first night was a bedlam of wailings and shriekings from hundreds of seal pups demanding the immediate return of mother.

Ah-Leek cried himself to sleep. He was hungry, but not so hungry that his thoughts turned to the food which could be caught in the clear cold waters of the sea. He wanted his mother to come. She *had* to come, or he would be hungry. He wanted rich, creamy milk, but that was something which he would never have again.

For a week, along with hundreds of other seal pups, he cried and wailed. Like the rest of them, Ah-Leek began to lose some of his butter-fat plumpness. Yet he did not go into the water. The sun was shining almost every day now, and though he was hungry he preferred to bask on the ice and join in the chorus of wails and shrieks. The idea of hunting for food had not occurred to any of them yet.

Then one day the sun did not shine. Dark clouds covered the sky, and a wind began to blow. As the wind grew to gale force the ice-field began to move even farther away from land. The lanes of water between the ice widened, then narrowed. They were like a flock of sheep jostling one another, and soon the air was filled not only with the scream of the storm but with the wild crunchings and crashings as ice-pans and larger floes ground against each other.

Ah-Leek lay on an ice-floe and gazed out into the grey world, not knowing what to do. The sea was not safe; for though he could hold his breath for quite a long time now, he dare not go into the water. He would have to surface now and then for breath, and might easily be killed if crushed between two ice-floes.

At length there was a tremendous bump as a larger floe ground against the ice-pan on which he had been resting. He was sent slithering for yards. As he scuttled back to a safer place he began to think for himself. He was growing up. He saw that the larger floe had a tangle of ice on it. Great lumps which had fallen off an even larger floe had formed into a kind of cave. It looked as if it would provide cover against the tearing anger of the wind. With a squeak of fear in case the two masses of ice should drift apart, he waddled across and got into the shelter.

He found a snug little corner among the masses of ice, and was shielded from the ripping torment of the wind. It was a lucky move, as hour by hour the wind blew even more strongly. For three days he huddled there while the ice-field crunched and ground itself into smaller and even smaller pieces. Then, quite quickly, the storm blew itself out.

Scores of seal pups had died during the storm, but Ah-Leek, though thinner and hungrier, was unharmed. He dropped off to sleep with the wind still screaming, and when he awoke there was an unbelievable calm over everything. The sun was shining on the open patches of water, and there was only the soft whisper of water lapping against ice. Quite suddenly Ah-Leek stopped worrying about his mother. The storm had driven all memory of her out of his mind.

Through a gap in his little ice-shelter he could see a most delightful scene; a dozen or more seal pups were playing together in the water. Like Ah-Leek, they had forgotten their sorrows, and each minute their cries attracted others. Ah-Leek gave a yelp of delight. He wanted to play with them, and it was only when he tried to reach the water that he discovered that something unexpected had happened during the storm.

The continual grinding of the ice-floe against other ice-floes had made the blocks of ice, which formed his shelter, settle closer. Now they were like a cave without a real door. There was an opening above him, but he could not climb the almost vertical ice wall. There were several small gaps through

which he could watch the other seal pups, but he could not get through.

Like a zoo tiger he waddled this way and that, bunting at the icy walls with his nose, scrabbling with a clumsy flipper at crevices which let in the sun, and finding none of them large enough to allow him through.

He was a prisoner, locked in an icy cell; and the only thing which could set him free was the sun—though by the time the sun melted the ice Ah-Leek would have died of starvation.

Pressing his nose to the largest of the cracks in the icy walls of his cell he called and called to the growing throng of seal pups. If they heard him they took no notice. Like a crowd of noisy school children waiting to start a picnic, the young seals were diving, splashing and shrieking, and one or two even trying to bark; while occasionally one of the cleverer ones would dive down and come to the surface with a fish in his jaws.

Ah-Leek watched them until just after noon. Then, as if someone had given a signal, the whole crowd of them began to swim westwards. It was as if a leader had decided that everyone was present and they might as well begin their journey.

From his prison Ah-Leek could only watch. He saw the mass of gently bobbing yellow and brown heads grow smaller and smaller. Then the leaders swung out of sight round a larger floe and within five minutes even the rearguard had gone.

Ah-Leek lay down, his nose still poking part way through

the gap in the ice. He was hungry and lonely, but suddenly he ceased his wild calling. He seemed to realize that it was no use wailing and shrieking. There was no one to hear him—no one to help him out of his prison.

He was not frightened, as a lost boy might be. He was not worried, for animals do not worry. He was getting quite accustomed to being hungry, though when he drifted off to sleep he gave an occasional twitch and whimper as he dreamed that his mother had returned, and that he was enjoying a long, rich feed of milk.

The seas were calm. There was no wind, and only an occasional big gull flew over. Ah-Leek spent most of the next day sleeping. There was nothing else to do. He could not hope to break out of his prison, and he did not know that a small army was on its way which would alter everything.

3

A Walrus Warrior

DAWN came just after three o'clock in the morning, and the first rays of the sun tipped every floating patch of ice with gold. The silence was broken, too, not by the screaming of sea birds, but by a queer 'singing' which gradually grew louder and louder.

Ah-Leek awoke as all children of the wild awake. One moment he was sound asleep and the next instant his eyes were wide and he was looking around. He stretched to flex his muscles, then licked at a tiny pool of melted ice water which had gathered near where he had been lying. He yawned mightily, showing a perfect set of tiny teeth in pink gums, then he was ready for whatever the new day might hold for him.

The 'singing' was growing quite loud now, and a few minutes later a creature such as he had never seen before swam into sight. It was a huge walrus bull, the leader of a herd on its annual migration to the west, and the Behring Sea.

Ah-Leek had never seen any animal so huge before. He was a curious pear shape, and when he heaved himself on to a nearby ice-floe he towered eight feet high. His curious bullet head, with its mat of stiff bristle whiskers, was adorned with two mighty down-curving tusks. They curved inwards, so that he had to hold his head slightly backwards to prevent his tusks stabbing into his chest.

Once on the floe he uttered a series of queer barking bellows, and within minutes there was a whole herd of walrus swimming towards the floe. They, like their leader, were brown, and all except the babies had tusks. They clambered on to the floe, and their weight was so great that it caused the mass of ice to tilt a little.

Ah-Leek watched them with interest. The mothers fed their babies, and for perhaps half an hour all were content to rest on the ice. They had been swimming steadily through the night, for they knew the danger of human hunters. Night time gave them a cloak of safety against the Eskimo hunters, who were now coming down to the beaches to hunt seal and walrus, as well as to catch fish to be dried for the coming winter.

At the end of half an hour first one then another of the walrus slid off the ice into the water. Each time showers of spray were thrown high and sparkled in the sunlight. The great brown animals went deep, for the walrus feed on clams and other shellfish which live on the sea bottom.

With their great curved tusks they scraped the mussels and clams from their holdfasts deep down, and as more and more of the herd went into the water the surface of the sea began to show signs of the feast which was going on down below.

Crunching shells between their powerful jaws as if they had

been no tougher than wafer biscuits, the walrus ate shellfish by the bucketful, and minute scraps of clams and mussels began to float to the surface.

Soon the sea was alive with small fish eagerly darting here and there to snap up the titbits. Only the babies and the big herd bull now remained on the big ice-floe. The walrus babies were asleep, but the mighty bull, his tusks gleaming in the sunshine, was alert and watchful. Propped up on his powerful fore flippers he was a real sentinel, his rather flat head turning this way and that. He watched all the channels between the ice-floes, to ensure that no enemy got near.

Yet, watchful master of the herd though he was, danger was drawing near which he neither saw nor heard. Miles away the sharp ears of a family of Eskimoes had caught the faint 'singing' of the herd. They knew that sound well enough, and there was rejoicing as they loaded their *umiak* (skin boat) and put out to sea.

The *umiak* was fitted with a modern outboard motor, but the men used long oar-like paddles. In a world so silent the sound of an outboard motor engine would have alarmed the walrus, and the herd could have swum away long before the men had a chance to use their guns.

They paddled quietly, pausing now and then to listen. A good haul of the massive walrus would ensure plenty to eat during the winter that was to come, and it was worth a lot of trouble to get close to the herd. In the *umiak*, which was quite a roomy vessel made of walrus skins stretched over a wooden framework, they also carried two of the sleek *kayaks*. These were one-man craft, slender and very light. In them a hunter could dart in and around the ice-floes with ease.

The chief hunter in the *umiak* called a halt when they were lucky enough to get a distant glimpse of the herd bull. They all listened, but now there was no 'singing' from the herd. The strange sound which many people say is like the singing of a distant choir is made when a herd of walrus are grunting and crying to one another. The mixture of sounds heard from a distance has a quality of singing about it which the Eskimo hunters know well.

Patiently the hunters, five men and a ten-year-old boy, waited. There was no point in getting closer until the herd had finished feeding. Once they got within range the object was to shoot as many walrus as possible, then get in close to prevent the huge bodies from sinking.

While the Eskimoes were waiting, Ah-Leek was lying flat on the ice and watching through a six-inch-wide gap in his prison wall. He knew it was no use struggling. Thick ice is far too strong for a young seal pup to claw through.

After a time the walrus began to clamber out on to the ice. They had kept bobbing up for breath, but now they were satisfied. The grown-up walrus could eat as much as four gallons of shellfish, which was one reason why a herd like this had always to be on the move. It did not take long to clear an area of sea bed when so many were eating so much at one time.

Finally most of the herd was back on the ice. Now it was time for the herd bull to feed, and he slithered into the water, making a tremendous splash. Down he went to satisfy his hunger, leaving a younger bull to act as sentinel. A hundred yards away, and hiding behind an ice floe, the Eskimo hunters listened while the 'singing' of the herd began again.

The oldest Eskimo picked up his paddle. They wasted no words. Each one knew by the sound that the herd had finished eating and would now be resting on the ice. With five guns they might be lucky and kill half a dozen walrus. If they did, then they would be happy indeed, for a full-grown walrus has as much meat on it as two big cows.

The ten-year-old boy, who had been named Andrew by a travelling missionary, though his Eskimo name meant 'Born-when-the-sun-came-to-life', sat in the stern, ready to take the steering-paddle when the shooting began. His eyes were alight with anticipation, for this was his first hunt. He was trying hard to hide his excitement, for even at ten years of age he felt that he was growing up.

Quietly the *umiak* was paddled round floe after floe until there was nothing else to hide them. Then, at a grunt from their leader, all five men dug their paddles deep and the light craft shot out into the open.

The watching bull was looking the other way; but something made him turn. He recognized the danger at once and gave the alarm. In a moment all was confusion. Mothers who had been settling down to sleep rolled upright, and with a heave of one powerful flipper started their children towards the sea.

The ice-floe rocked under the sudden movement and that helped the herd. The movement of the floe sent heavy ripples outwards which caused the *umiak* to bob unexpectedly, and the first bullets went wide. By the time the men were steadying themselves, more and more walrus were plunging into the sea, sending spray flying in all directions.

Ah-Leek blinked and cringed at the sharp, whip-like reports of the rifles. He drew back even more as a bullet ricocheted off the place on which the walrus had been resting, and crashed into the ice close to him. It sent dazzling white splinters into the air.

Splash . . . splash . . . splash! The huge brown bodies tumbled helter-skelter into the water. Great masses of spray were thrown into the air, making it difficult for the men to see where to shoot. One bullet found a target. The leader of the Eskimoes was a crack shot, and his first bullet killed an old animal so cleanly that it died without knowing what had happened. The other hunters were less lucky.

Within ninety seconds the ice was clear, save for that one dead animal; and the sea was a heaving froth of foam. Mothers took their babies deep down; but one baby slipped from his mother's grasp and shot up to the surface again. For a moment or so he bobbed about, then his mother came up to save him.

She came to the surface less than ten yards from the rocking *umiak*, where the hunters were reloading their still smoking guns. One of the men saw her and shouted. He swung his gun to his shoulder, and as he did so the old herd leader came up from below.

The big bull walrus had just begun to feed and was happily crunching a clam, when through the water came the sound of many of the herd diving. The succession of 'plops' told him at once that his family was in trouble, and looking up through the crystal-clear water he saw the shape of the *umiak*.

He knew all about boats like this, and the pain which could follow. As a much younger bull he had been wounded in the shoulder by a badly aimed bullet, which was one reason why he was so cautious when leading his family along the coast.

The moment he caught sight of the underside of the boat he spat out the clam and with tremendously powerful strokes of his fore flippers raced upwards. His strength was amazing and his speed hard to believe. Faster than a rising air-bubble he went. Dark shapes were coming down towards him as the herd dived for safety. Skilfully he swept by them, and came up under the boat with a force which, hitting the main bottom strut, splintered it, and tore a hole in the walrus-hide hull.

The herd bull was dazed by the blow, but his action had saved the mother and her baby. The man with the rifle was just squeezing the trigger and the distance was so short that he could hardly have missed. Then the *umiak* heaved under him with sudden violence. His gun boomed, but the bullet went harmlessly high into the air.

A moment later the five men were tumbled in a heap, while water spouted over them from the gash in the bottom of their boat. Within seconds the big walrus bull came in view. The mother had grabbed her baby under one big flipper and was plunging out of sight. Roaring defiance, the bull reared up out of the water, hooked his long tusks over the gunwale of the *umiak* and then flung himself backwards.

It was a clever move; had it succeeded the side would have been torn out of the Eskimoes' craft, and the hunters would have been flung into the icy water. The bull almost succeeded, and it was the boy who foiled him. He had been sitting in the stern, his hands on the steering-paddle. So, though their frail craft rocked so mightily and threw the rest of the crew off balance, he managed to keep his place.

While his father, grandfather and the three other men floundered in the bottom of the *umiak* the boy got to his feet. He was pale beneath the ruddy tan which sun-glare off the ice gives to the Eskimos; but he had lots of courage. Lifting the steering-paddle he struck a mighty blow at the walrus bull's head.

The blow missed, for the bull heaved upwards as the paddle came down—a move which unhooked his tusks from the side of the boat. Then he disappeared in a swirl of icy water.

As he took his great weight off the *umiak* it rocked wildly. Andrew was not prepared for that, and with a yell of terror he fell over the side, throwing spray a yard high.

Ah-Leek saw it all, but he was not very interested. He had never seen men before, and imagined the boat was some new kind of sea animal, perhaps a new kind of walrus. Nor did he quiver with excitement when he saw the Eskimoes seize their paddles and begin stabbing at the water in an effort to get their sinking craft to the side of the floe where the walrus had been basking only a few minutes earlier.

What *did* interest him, however, was the battle which began a few moments later. He saw the water splash up as the

Eskimo boy fell into the sea, and some twenty seconds later the youngster reappeared. Then, shooting up to the surface again like a huge cork, came the big bull walrus.

Coming up between boy and the rest of the Eskimoes the herd bull considered which to attack. The five men were struggling frantically to get their damaged *umiak* to the ice-floe, and they were making a lot of noise and splashing the water vigorously. They were doing this to discourage the big herd bull from returning to the attack, and they succeeded.

With a grunt the walrus turned away and ploughed through the icy water in pursuit of Andrew. The youngster was panting and terrified. He could swim, but his heavy clothing hampered every movement. He wore the usual Eskimo waterproof seal-skin boots, thick trousers and a parka. The parka was like a big loose shirt with no buttons, and a heavy fur-trimmed hood which could fit over the wearer's head in windy weather.

Luckily for Andrew, the ice-floe on which Ah-Leek was a prisoner was no more than twenty yards away, though if the walrus bull had started to chase the boy immediately he came to the surface he would have caught him without any difficulty. As it was, though he was panting wildly, the youngster managed to scramble on to the ice no more than a second or so ahead of his pursuer.

There was a frightening crash as the walrus reared out of the water and brought down his curved tusks into the ice only a few inches behind Andrew. It was such a savage blow that ice-chips flew in all directions, and for a moment or so it seemed as if the walrus himself had been made prisoner. His sharp tusks had dug two holes and remained embedded in the ice.

Andrew, water streaming from his clothes, crawled a few feet away and lay face down, panting for breath. Then, as he heard a frightening grunt from the edge of the ice-floe, he lifted himself up and looked back. What he saw would have frightened the bravest of the brave. The walrus bull had got his tusks free and was heaving himself on to the ice.

For a moment Andrew almost gave himself up for lost. The ice-floe was not a large one, and his knees were already shaking from weakness. The huge walrus was a towering monster whose strength was as great as ever. He could waddle round the ice-floe in pursuit of the boy until the young Eskimo dropped from weariness, or dived into the sea. If he did that nothing could save him.

Then, as he struggled to his feet, Andrew heard a frightened wail. It came from Ah-Leek, still penned in his icy prison. The blocks of ice which kept him from reaching the sea were lying against one another like a pile of huge play-bricks, and there was a gap in the top. Ah-Leek had seen the gap, but had been unable to climb to freedom that way. Now he lay as close to the ice as he could, afraid of the big bull and equally afraid of Andrew.

In desperation the young Eskimo hurled himself at the six-foot-high mound of ice. He found a crevice with his fingers and heaved himself over the top. It was the nearest he had ever been to sudden death, for the angry bull again sent chips of ice flying as his tusks dug in only inches behind where Andrew had been.

Ah-Leek squealed in fright as the exhausted and terrified boy dropped down almost on him. There was no room to back away, for the prison was an icy chamber of only some five feet by four feet.

Andrew flopped on his face and lay gasping. Ah-Leek stared at him, and then turned his head as he saw through the ice the shadow of the big walrus. Weighing more than a ton and possessing the strength of a dozen men, he waddled round the mound of ice, roaring in his rage. Then he saw the gap through which Ah-Leek had watched the happenings of the past few minutes.

The young seal backed away at sight of the fiercely whiskered face of the big walrus bull. Then, urged on by the scent of Andrew, the walrus inserted a big flipper into the gap in the ice-blocks and, by chance rather than design, he dislodged one.

There was a sudden crunching of ice against ice as the blocks moved. One toppled over, and a moment later the prison was no longer a prison. There was a gap through which Ah-Leek could have got to the sea quite easily, if the walrus had not barred the way.

In sudden alarm the walrus scuttled away when the ice-blocks began to slide, but now he blocked the way to freedom. He stood there, looking gigantic as he reared up on his hind flippers, his tusks like twin swords. Walrus are usually good-tempered creatures, but this herd bull was now in the mood to kill and kill. His family had been attacked, and he meant to have revenge.

When the last ice-block settled again the walrus waddled

forward, and with no escape Ah-Leek set up a terrified wailing. For a moment the angry bull hesitated, then came on. He had got the scent of Andrew, and the smell of humans always enraged him. One fierce downward jab with his tusks would give him revenge, and a second thrust would put Ah-Leek out of his misery.

4

A Cry for Help

ON THE fifty yards distant ice-floe Andrew's father, grandfather and the three other men were hastily emptying their gear out of the damaged *umiak*. They were all wet to the knees and all panting for breath. It had been a struggle to get on to the floe without losing the boat and the precious rifles.

Then Andrew's grandfather looked up, and his eyes widened in alarm as he asked:

'Where is the boy?'

In the rush and excitement of the past minutes each man had been too busy to think of their ten-year-old passenger. Now they looked around, as if they half expected him to be standing behind someone.

Andrew's father opened his mouth in horror, but no sound came. He looked off the ice at the sunlit water. There was now no sign of the walrus herd. Once they had got below the surface of the sea they had swum swiftly away, coming up only when they could see other ice-floes above them. The only evidence that there had been a herd was the dead walrus on the floe some few yards away from the hunters. There was no sign of Andrew.

Then on the silent air came a wailing cry. It might have been made by a two-year-old human baby, and it caused the five Eskimoes to swing round and stare in the direction from which the sound came.

Accustomed to danger though they were, the sight which met their eyes brought gasps from them. The big bull walrus, black against the blue-green of the ice, was moving in to a tumble of ice and it was from this direction that the wail of terror had come.

'It is the boy!' one of the men gasped, and grabbed for a rifle. Andrew's father was even quicker. He whipped up his gun, cocked it and fired. He did not waste time trying to shoot the walrus.

Crack! In the profound silence which lay over everything the report was like a blast of thunder, and the sound was flung backwards and forwards in a score of echoes from the many ice-floes.

Crack . . . crack . . . crack . . . crack . . . crack! All these sounds came from the ice-floes, quick-fire echoes of the actual shot.

Then another man fired, this time aiming at the walrus.

Ah-Leek, whose cry had given the alarm, was watching with bulging eyes as the big brown herd bull lunged forward to get within striking distance of the Eskimo boy. Then came the strange reports, and a few moments later a bullet struck the ice only an inch or so from the walrus bull's head.

He gave a mighty bellow of rage, heaved himself backwards, and then there was a tremendous splash as he flung himself into the sea. He remembered the days of long ago when, after just such a report, there had been a biting pain in his shoulder where a bullet had lodged. Memory brought fear and his anger evaporated. Revenge was forgotten, and once the sea engulfed him he did not come to the surface again until he had joined his family a quarter of a mile away.

Ah-Leek waited for more than a minute, all the time expecting to see the dark brown body of the walrus bull rise to the surface again. The ripples he had made when he splashed in smoothed away, and everything became strangely still and quiet. Suddenly realizing that he could escape, Ah-Leek flopped through the gap in the ice-blocks and hurried towards the edge of the floe. It seemed a long time since he had felt the coolness of the sea round him. He had completely forgotten how he had cried for his mother; but hunger was not easy to forget, and he was going to fish. He was making a little mewing noise in his eagerness, happy to be free.

Some fifty yards away the Eskimo hunters clustered on the edge of their floe. They were waiting for young Andrew to come out from the jumbled mass of ice into which they had seen the walrus forcing his way.

'Here he is,' Andrew's grandfather said thankfully as a dark form was seen. Then Ah-Leek shuffled into the open. Sight of him drew grunts of disgust from the watchers, and a groan of despair from Andrew's father. Each of them realized in that moment where the piping wail had come from. It had not been Andrew, but this seal.

One of the men lifted his rifle in sudden anger and, taking

quick aim, fired. Ah-Leek never knew what happened. One moment he was within a few feet of the sunlit water, the next moment everything was inky black. The bullet had just touched him on top of the head.

The wound was no more than a scratch, and would quickly heal when it was immersed in salt water. The immediate effect, however, was to put the young seal into a quick sleep. He flopped down and did not even wriggle.

'A bullet for a baby seal!' one of the others said. 'That is a waste.'

There were grunts from the others, and laying down their rifles they busied themselves with the task of mending the slit in their walrus-skin boat. They were quick and skilful. At one time they would have used bone needles, but now they could buy slender steel needles from a trading post, and the work was better done.

They lowered their craft into the water, grunting as they saw that the patch leaked only very slightly. They then got on with the task of skinning the dead walrus and cutting up the meat. It was done swiftly and with great skill. In half an hour the task was finished and their prize loaded into the damaged *umiak*. It sank lower in the water and, where they had sewn up the tear, water spurted up.

Then the man who had shot Ah-Leek said: 'We may as well pick up the baby seal. I used a bullet on him.'

The others nodded. Four men picked up paddles. The fifth man began to bale as more water spurted in along the seams of the patch in the bottom. They swept smoothly across the water, and came alongside the floe on which Ah-Leek still lay. They had thought him dead, but consciousness was returning and already he was beginning to move a little.

Andrew's father and another man got on to the ice. The older man held the rope which kept their craft to the side of the floe. The other man drew his knife to finish off the young seal and skin it.

He was reaching down to grab Ah-Leek when, out of the corner of his eyes, he saw a vague shadow move within the circle of ice-blocks. It was Andrew, only half conscious, but struggling to get to his father after hearing voices. He was too dazed from exhaustion and cold to speak, but his slight movements were seen. For a moment the Eskimo was too startled to move, then he gave a great cry of:

'He is here! Andrew is here. The boy is not drowned. Look, Andrew is alive!'

They dragged the boy out of the jumble of ice-blocks, pummelled him, slapped his face, rubbed him vigorously, and finally saw the eyes open for a moment. Then the face which had been turning blue-grey creased into a weak smile.

'He lives!' Andrew's father shouted joyfully. 'Into the *umiak* with him. We must get him ashore. Father . . . the Great Spirit has been good to us this day, and Andrew's mother will not weep tonight.'

They carried the moaning youngster to the edge of the floe and lowered him into the *umiak*; then the man who had been about to finish off Ah-Leek drew his knife again.

'It will not take a minute,' he said. 'And a baby seal is worth taking back.'

'Wait!' It was Andrew's grandfather. His face was wrinkled, and his eyes were slanted almost like the eyes of a Mongolian. He was old, and the most experienced hunter of them all, so the others listened to him with respect. 'Is it good to kill when my grandson would be dead if the seal pup had not cried out?'

His companions stared at him, frowning. Up here, where men depended on their hunting skill for food, even a young seal was worth taking home. It seemed silly not to kill when the pup was lying to hand. They looked at him in surprise, and none of them spoke.

'Why did you fire your gun?' the old man asked, turning to Andrew's father.

'Because I heard a cry, and thought it was Andrew calling for help.'

'And because you fired, the bull walrus left Andrew. So the boy is alive,' was the quiet reply. 'We thought he had been drowned. If this seal pup had not broken the silence we would never have found your son. Put the seal into the *umiak*. If he is badly hurt, then we can kill him later. If he is . . . ah!' He stopped, for Ah-Leek had opened his big baby eyes and, regaining full consciousness, rolled off his side into a position where he could get into the sea, if his captors allowed him to move.

'It is foolish to waste good meat,' the man who had shot Ah-Leek grumbled.

'For the life of my grandson I would pay more than one seal pup,' Andrew's grandfather said soberly. 'Push the pup into the sea. If he swims well . . . he can go. If he is crippled . . . well, it will be kinder to kill him.'

Ah-Leek gave a shriek as he was grabbed and bundled to the edge of the floe, but a moment later, with a little splash, he was in the water. The shock of the sudden cold all over his body drove the last dizziness from his head, and with a quick twist and a powerful stroke from his flippers he dived deep.

Andrew's grandfather tugged at the few long hairs on his chin which he called a beard, and nodded thoughtfully.

'It is always good to repay a debt,' he said. 'To that seal pup we owe young Andrew. Now let us paddle home. The women will be waiting, and there will be much fresh meat for our bellies when the cooking-fires die down. This day the sea has been kind to us, and given back the son we thought was dead. What is the loss of one seal pup? There are many thousands of seals in the sea—but there is only one boy of our blood named Andrew.'

Frowns gave way to smiles. The boy was moved gently into the bows and, while his grandfather busied himself chafing his arms and legs to keep the blood circulating, the others dipped their paddles. The man who was baling worked as hard as anyone, for more and more water seemed to be spurting up through the patch.

Miles away now the herd of walrus were climbing out on to another ice-floe, and the herd bull, though he was still hungry, found a vantage point where he could watch for the approach of enemies. When the babies were young, being the master of the herd was a hard life.

Down below, in a world he had almost forgotten, Ah-Leek was looking for food. He was a lonely seal pup in waters where there were no other seals. They had all swum westwards on the annual migration—mothers first, babies almost two weeks later.

Something inside Ah-Leek would force him to swim westwards in search of the others, but for the moment his one thought was food. He was lean and hungry.

5

Ah-Leek the Lonely

THERE was no shortage of food for the quick-moving hunter, for even when the ice covered the sea right to the land there were fish in the dark waters. Now, with spring here, that life seemed suddenly to have increased a hundred-fold. It was as if some huge pan had boiled over, spilling fish by the million into the cold clear seas.

From much farther south a gigantic army of herring was moving into the cold northern waters. They were looking for shallows where they could lay their sticky batches of eggs on something which would hold fast until they hatched out. The herring seemed to know that the summer in this part of the world was very short and, if their babies were to hatch out, and learn how to avoid being eaten by their enemies, they would have to be hatched out soon. Within two months the ice would begin forming again, and soon afterwards the sun would be gone for another long winter of bitter cold and mighty winds.

The herring were moving towards a place where a great river emptied into the sea. The river would wash down trees, broken branches, all kinds of debris to which a mother herring could attach her eggs. And this vast multitude of grey and blue striped fish were nearing the shores when Ah-Leek found his freedom.

He had chased an elusive tom-cod until he was tired and breathless; but he had no success. Not until he had got back some of his strength would he be swift enough to outswim most fishes. He drifted to the surface to breathe, and when he swept below again the sea, which had seemed almost empty, was now filled.

Like a million bars of grey-green and blue the advance guard of the herrings were moving shorewards. They ranged from about twenty feet from the surface to as far down as the clear water would allow the young seal to see. How many million herrings there were in the shoal no man would ever know.

Ah-Leek was not concerned with how many there were. He wanted one to begin with, and like a grey-brown torpedo he dived into the fringes of the shoal. The herrings scattered, up, down, sideways; but there were too many for Ah-Leek not to succeed this time.

Within a minute he was shooting to the surface, a herring weighing almost a pound in his jaws. He tossed it neatly into the air, caught it by the head and swallowed it. Why he did that he did not know; yet it was the only way to deal with a herring. If he had started to swallow it by the tail the fins, which are made to fold alongside the fish's body, would have been forced out, and his meal would have stuck in his throat.

He ate and ate until even his weeks' long hunger was satisfied. Then he swam to an ice-pan, climbed on to it, and basked in the sunshine. He should have been happy, for he was free, and full fed. Yet now that his hunger was gone he felt there was something wrong. He did not know quite what it was, and after only a few minutes in the sunshine he slithered into the sea again.

The vast shoal of herring was still moving steadily towards the shallower waters, but he was not interested in them now. He swam a few feet below the surface, while a few feet below him the millions of fish, like a huge army, went on and on.

A fishing vessel with the right kind of nets could have filled her holds to bursting in an hour or so; but no fishing vessel ever came to these northern waters. Nature guarded the herring. The treacherous ice-floes moved about at the whim of tide and wind. In addition there were sudden sea fogs. The sun could be shining brilliantly, but in an hour everything could be shrouded in a cold grey mist. So, except for the few which went to feed seals like Ah-Leek, the herring got close to the shore and laid their eggs.

The seal pup swam for half an hour before he had crossed the great belt of herring. When he did finally leave them behind the sea seemed almost empty. There were pollock and tom-cod below him, and above the sea were the birds. He was coming to a place where one or two rocky islets lay offshore, and these were white with sea birds.

Twice Ah-Leek was startled by a sudden splash in the water ahead of him as a sea bird dived. Then he came on a family of eider duck. They were not yet ready for laying their eggs, and ducks and drakes played together.

As Ah-Leek swam near, the eiders, who had been providing a chorus of musical sounds like 'A-uh—a-uhu . . . a-uh—a-uuh', tipped up their tails and dived. Ah-Leek sank beneath the surface as well.

He saw the eiders moving like beautifully coloured bullets, streaming a thousand tiny air-bubbles from their feathers as they chased among a school of small fish which had swum close.

With their wings pressed close to their beautifully shaped bodies the eiders raced along, propelled by fast-moving webbed feet. Ah-Leek was suddenly excited. He was beginning to feel hungry again, and with smooth movements of his flippers went in pursuit of the nearest eider duck.

It was like chasing a ghost. The moment he drew near the duck she changed direction, shot to the surface, and as he made a lunge for one of her webbed feet her powerful wings lifted her into the air, and out of his reach. Ah-Leek, enjoying the game, turned and lunged through the water as another eider duck popped to the surface, a long lugworm dangling on each side of his bill.

It was like playing blind-man's-buff. The eider duck turned, skittered along the surface for a yard or so, her webbed feet making tiny patterns on the water, and then it too was gone.

Ah-Leek lay still in the water for a few minutes. He was very young, and desperately wanted someone to play with. At the end of half an hour he began swimming westwards. Why he went westwards, following the main body of seal pups, he did not know; but it was something he just *had* to do.

Though he was unaware of it, there was a very powerful reason why all the seals should leave this part of the northern waters. The mothers and fathers were already enjoying themselves on lonely beaches guarded by rugged cliffs. The seal pups would play about on other beaches and in the shallow waters—and it was the shallow waters which kept them from harm.

About this time of the year whales appeared off the coasts; many of them had baby whales with them, and following them came the tigers of the sea—schools of killer whales.

The killer whales were not so large as ordinary whales, but they were as bloodthirsty and ferocious as a pack of starving wolves. Sighting a school of ordinary, rather slow-moving whales, they would charge in like dogs chasing a frightened cat. Their teeth were interlocking, and they could tear a sixty-foot whale to pieces very quickly.

Seals moved westwards to be out of the way when the killer whales arrived, but Ah-Leek had been delayed. By the time he began his long swim to the west the hunters had arrived, and at this time of the year they were usually ravenous. Even a baby seal was not too small a morsel to be left in peace.

Unaware of the dangers towards which he was swimming the young seal headed west, and was delighted when he saw ahead of him a whale mother and her calf. Even the calf was large enough to make Ah-Leek seem no more than a sprat in the sea; but the huge mother and her son were so happy together that they took no notice of the young seal.

So lonely that he was glad of any company, Ah-Leek swam

alongside the mother and her baby. The whale looked at him for a moment, ready to strike out with one of her huge flippers if he should prove to be an enemy. Then, as she recognized him, she dipped below the surface, taking her baby down with her.

Ah-Leek followed them, anxious to stay with any sea creature which would be friendly. The sea was some sixty feet deep here, and the bottom was covered with rubbery bladder-wrack which waved to and fro as the whales disturbed the water.

Even down at sixty feet the water was so crystal clear that the sunlight could penetrate, to show what was going on in this strange world. A starfish was huddled over a mussel patiently trying to force open the shell. It was a silent fight for life. If the starfish won there would soon be an empty mussel shell drifting with the tide. If the mussel was strong enough then the starfish would swim away hungry, and look for an easier meal.

There were toad crabs which were hard to distinguish when they were at rest, for each carried on the top of his shell a miniature garden of tiny fronds of sea grass. Once the crabs came to rest they were almost invisible, for the grass mingled with that already growing on the sea bed.

Everywhere the dwellers in the deep had some defence against their natural enemies. Some relied on speed to get them away from an enemy. Some could drop down to the sandy bottom and with a wriggle or two sink into the sand and out of sight. Ah-Leek was one of the few with little defence against an attacker.

If he basked on an ice-floe he was at the mercy of any marauding polar bear who saw him. The polar bears were powerful swimmers, and cunning. Usually they hid in ice-floes or would swim near, under water, and come up with a rush. However, Nature had given Ah-Leek one compensation: a poor memory. Though he had wailed for a week for his mother, he had now forgotten her completely. He had also forgotten the hard days he had spent as a lonely prisoner in the ice-cell. Even the appearance of the Eskimo boy Andrew was fading out of his mind.

Within minutes of escaping from some terrible danger he could forget it and be happy. Though he did not know it, danger was coming very close even as he swam about near the forty-ton whale and her four-ton baby.

The mother whale drifted up to the surface, and the moment her single nostril was clear of the water she blew out a jet of fine spray. Her baby did the same, and the two monsters lay there recharging their mighty lungs with oxygen. Ah-Leek swam close to the baby, looking up at what to him was a huge mass of blubber.

All was quiet and peaceful until, through the water—which carries sounds in waves for great distances—came a peculiar vibration. It was almost as if some giant was beating the surface of the sea with a huge paddle.

Ah-Leek felt the vibrations, but they meant nothing to him. They meant a great deal to the mother whale. She had a good memory for any sound which spelled danger, and the *thump, thump* announced the approach of a school of the dreaded killer whales. From them there were only two methods of escape. One was to dive deep and remain near the sea bed. In this way the 'killers' might pass overhead, unaware that the whales were hiding beneath them. The other way was to go into shallow waters. Killer whales would seldom approach the shore. They were afraid of being stranded. Shallows were a danger, too, for the whales, and the mother decided to dive.

Down she went, taking her baby with her. Ah-Leek was not the least frightened by the steady beat as a dozen killer whales rushed westwards, swinging up out of the depths like porpoises. They raced along like a well-drilled platoon of soldiers, and it was this shooting half out of the water which sent the warning vibrations along to such creatures as the whale and her young one.

The young seal followed the two whales down to the sea bed and cruised to and fro around them. His nostrils were pinched shut and his mouth was tight closed. He could stay below for some time; but not for as long as a whale. One thing he noticed, as he swam past the mother, and that was the vibrations which came from her.

Terror was making the mother's heart beat much quicker than usual, and it was sending tiny vibrations through the icy depths. Luckily for her the quick beating of her heart was covered up by the strong *bump-bump, bump-bump* which came from the hunters up above.

The school of killer whales was very near now. They swam as if they were in a race, and might almost have been a pack of hounds following the scent of a tired fox. They passed overhead, and would have gone on much farther before turning back if Ah-Leek had not surfaced.

He had kept close to the mother whale and her baby, expecting them to begin rising for air; but they had filled their huge lungs with oxygen, and if need be could stay under water for fifteen to twenty minutes. Ah-Leek could not remain without breath for so long.

Reluctantly, though he was growing uneasy at the steady pulse-beat from above, he shot upwards. He had remained below longer than usual, and needed air quickly.

He popped up out of the water, his yellow-brown head glinting wetly in the sunshine—and not fifty yards away, and heading almost directly for him, was the leader of the killers.

A slight flick of his mighty tail turned the killer whale, and he rushed for the seal pup. His eyes gleamed coldly and his mouth was slightly open, revealing his teeth. Like the rest of his school he was hungry, and though Ah-Leek would hardly be a mouthful, he was not in the mood to pass even a snack. The others in the school also changed direction as Ah-Leek hurriedly filled his lungs then turned and dived again for the sea bed.

Above him there was a series of roaring thuds as ten great killer whales upended their bodies and raced after him. They left the surface of the sea agitated into a mass of milky foam, towards which a big robber gull raced, thinking something must have died there, and there would be a free feast for him.

6

Battle Royal

AH-LEEK'S heart was thumping wildly as he went down like a torpedo for the bottom. He had never seen killer whales before, but the one glance he had got of open mouths and rows of teeth had been enough for him. There was something terrifying about them which made him swim faster than he had ever swum before.

Even so he would have lost the race but for the whale below. She knew all about the dark-blue-and-white hunters. She could tell what was happening by the vibrations coming through the water, and with a baby to protect she did not wait to be caught on the bottom of the sea.

Ah-Leek never saw her. He dare not look behind, but could tell by the swift and strong paddle-beat strokes that the killers were gaining on him. The leader was no more than six feet from him when out of the depths came the dark shape of the mother whale.

By some means she had ordered the baby to stay on the bottom, and she rose up to meet the danger. Normally quiet and peaceful, there was no risk she would not face to keep her baby out of danger. As she charged upwards, driven by the might of her powerful flippers, Ah-Leek went past and turned only just in time to avoid crashing nose on to the baby whale.

He swerved and, turning on his side, looked upwards. In a matter of seconds the situation had changed. The downward rush of the ten killer whales had been reversed. The leader had come almost face to face with the whale, and he had attacked at once.

He took one swift slashing bite at her, then was struck a tremendous blow on the ribs by the whale's left flipper, and from that moment the hunters needed a new leader. The killer whale's back was broken, and he drifted upwards, his white underparts glinting in the sunshine when he broke surface.

The other nine did not spare a second glance for their dead leader, but plunged in. They could swim much quicker than the whale, but got in each other's way. The whale, ponderous creature though she was, and weighing as much as a small railway engine, flung herself clear out of the water.

It would have been an amazing sight for any man lucky enough to have seen it, but the only spectators were a few brown-bodied walrus dozing on an ice-floe a quarter of a mile away.

Nine killer whales leapt half their length out of the water in pursuit, and the sea was threshed to milky foam. A moment later the forty-ton whale came down with a tremendous crash which sent hundreds of gallons of water splashing high in the sunshine.

For the next quarter of an hour the battle went on without pause. Two more killer whales were either killed or so badly

injured that they could take no further part in the battle. But the mother whale was being worn down. She was bleeding from a dozen places where the slashing teeth had gripped her for a moment.

Feeling her strength fading, she summoned up one last burst of energy. She knew exactly where she had left her baby, and she knew that the youngster would have been forced to come up for air by this time.

In an effort to save him she had carried the fight farther and farther from that place. Now, growing weary, she decided to return. Striking another of her attackers a blow with one of her flippers she started to swim back to the spot where the fight had begun.

Half a mile away the baby whale and Ah-Leek were just surfacing for air. The young whale had obeyed the orders from his mother to stay in that one place, and Ah-Leek was glad enough to stay as well. He had not yet got over the fright the killer whales had given him, and felt secure with his much larger companion.

The young whale lay on the surface, filling and emptying his lungs in the crisp, pure air. After a few minutes' breathing like this he could sink to the bottom and stay there, if need be, for another twenty minutes. Ah-Leek was not so fortunate. He could stay under for a few minutes, then he must come up for air.

Suddenly they realized that the vibrations coming to them through the water were louder and drawing nearer. The fight to the death, which had gradually moved away, was now coming back—and coming back swiftly. The young whale sank quietly down to the sea bed. Ah-Leek followed, and they lay there for six or seven minutes.

There had been another skirmish on the surface, the mother whale turning on her pursuers. Three times she had hurled her vast bulk out of the water as one of the killer whales got a grip on her. Three times she had beaten off her attackers. Now, desperately weary, she was forcing herself into a last mad dash towards her baby son.

Ah-Leek was beginning to feel the need for air. He swam slowly round the young whale, waiting for him to rise; but there was no movement at all. Young though he was, the baby whale felt that the safest place for him was down here on the bed of the sea. He could remain below for another ten or fifteen minutes.

Finally, when his lungs were beginning to hurt, Ah-Leek shot surfacewards. He had to breathe or die. He was afraid now, for the sea was bringing the *throb-throb-throb* of the killer whales' flukes ever more strongly. They were very near!

As he shot upwards through the amazingly clear water, Ah-Leek saw the huge bulk of the mother whale sliding along overhead. Her normal speed was about five miles an hour. Now, despite her weariness and the savage wounds she had suffered, she was moving at almost twice that speed. She had meant to return to her baby, but remembered at the very last moment that if she called him up he would most certainly die. She was going on, hoping to draw the killer pack away.

Behind her, and also growing weary, came five of the blue-white hunters. They had not got off scot-free in the battle and, though they were desperately hungry, they were content for the moment to keep some forty yards behind their intended victim. They were waiting until sheer weariness forced her to stop. Then they would close in.

Ah-Leek bobbed up just behind the mother whale. His lungs were aching to be emptied, and he gave a huge sigh of relief when he got rid of the stale air and sucked in a fresh supply which was cold and invigorating, and filled with life-giving oxygen.

He was emptying his lungs again when he realized the killer whales were almost on him. The nearest was no more than twenty yards away, and surging along like a power-boat under full throttle.

If he had been older and more experienced Ah-Leek would have turned nose down and swum for the bottom. Below the surface he could have dodged this way and that much more quickly than his ten-ton enemies. Instead of doing the right thing he panicked.

He turned and swam off to one side, hoping the killer pack would pass him by. It was a mistake. The little splash of foam he kicked up caught the eye of the foremost of the blue-white hunters, and he turned in pursuit. He had not forgotten the whale, but thought that he could snatch a quick mouthful to take the edge off his grinding hunger.

The other killer whales turned automatically, and had there

been an observer he would have witnessed the strange sight of five powerful killer whales in hot pursuit of a frightened, very tiny seal pup.

For perhaps twenty seconds Ah-Leek managed to hold his own, but he was young and his muscles were not toughened up. His speed began to decrease. The tremendous threshing of water behind him grew louder and louder as the five massive killer whales drew in.

On the sea bed crabs froze to immobility, while their eyes-on-stalks probed upwards. Never before had they seen killer whales charging through the shallow waters as now. They saw the slim torpedo shape of the seal pup in the lead, but the gap between hunted and hunters dwindled quickly.

Ah-Leek's heart was almost bursting with terror and the tremendous effort he was making. His flippers moved so quickly that they sent tiny corkscrews of water seething upwards.

He was so terror-filled that he did not see the dark shape ahead of him until he was on it. His fore flippers struck something solid, he was lifted up above the surface, water being thrown off his round, shining head in a multitude of tiny droplets which shone like jewels in the sunshine.

He turned his head, and the nearest killer whale was less than a dozen feet away. Ah-Leek tried to swim, but suddenly there was no water beneath him, and he flopped down, his lungs pumping madly. He had lost his first race for life!

7

Guardians of the Beach

WHATEVER Ah-Leek was expecting to happen did not take place. He lay there and the wet sand throbbed and trembled as if half a dozen mad drummers were beating it with mighty drumsticks. The young seal lay and gasped, afraid to open his eyes—afraid even to move, while the frantic thrumming went on and on.

Gradually Ah-Leek's racing heart-beat slowed down. He opened his eyes and heaved himself up on his fore flippers. Something very strange had happened. It was something he did not understand, though the answer was simple enough. When he turned aside, hoping to get out of the path of the five killer whales, he had headed for land.

They had been opposite where a small stream came out into the sea, and it had built up a sand bar which was partially covered at high tide. The tide was going out when Ah-Leek encountered the strange shadow—which was nothing more than a wide ridge of sand just below the surface. It was the sand bar which had forced him out of the water.

Lying on the ridge of sand, with the tide flowing out and exposing a little more sand every minute, he looked back towards the frantic drumming. The sight which met his big, bulging baby eyes sent him squeaking off the sand towards the shore at once.

In line, and spaced out at seven-yard intervals, were the five killer whales. Their eagerness to make a kill had blinded them to the dangers of the shallowing water. Before they could stop they had charged headlong on to the beginning of the sand bar, and now they were stranded.

Vainly they were threshing the inches-deep water with their mighty flukes, trying to drive themselves back to deeper water. All they were succeeding in doing, however, was to churn up sand and water into a thin porridge mixture, and dig a groove into which their mighty bodies were slowly sinking deeper and deeper.

Ah-Leek scuttled ashore in the peculiar lolloping movement which belongs to the seal on land, his flippers leaving a strange trail on the damp sand. Not until he drew near a four-foot bank, which was the land proper, did he stop and look back.

The five killer whales were still in the same place. They were still threshing wildly, though not with the same vigour as before. The water was leaving them, and even in this short space of time they were beginning to feel the effects of the sun on their backs. It was drying and tightening their skin, and they were too hot. Without the chill of icy water on them they were suffering a rise in temperature. They were like children who have played out in the hot sun for too long, and were suddenly feeling very sick.

There was a final spasmodic threshing as they felt the tide leaving them more and more, then the struggles died away.

Ah-Leek watched from the shelter of the overhanging bank. He wanted to get down to the sea. He was hungry again, and with the herring shoals still coming in towards the shallows there was unlimited food for the taking; but he was afraid of those five motionless forms. They seemed to be watching him: waiting for him to try to return to the sea. For him they spelled danger.

Nor could he skirt round them. He did cross the stream, but there was a tangle of stunted trees growing along the river bank, and he was afraid to try to force his way through them. Reluctantly he returned to the beach, but the killers were still there. He was marooned until they left.

The sun dropped slowly towards the horizon, and soon the stars came out. The night was bitterly cold, but he did not feel the bite of it. He still had an inch of blubber beneath his skin; and this kept the cold at bay.

Finding a sheltered spot he dozed, waking in the middle of the night when he heard a grunting noise, and a creaking among the brushwood across the narrow stream. It was a cow caribou, and in the quiet of the night she gave birth to a calf.

It was the time for the coming to life of new young things;

but the loving little sounds the mother caribou made as she licked her calf from head to foot kept Ah-Leek awake, tense and frightened.

As the dawn came in he moved down towards the beach, and in the half light saw that the five blue-white killer whales were still where he had last seen them. Disappointed, he turned back. He crossed the stream, only to be confronted by a frightened but determined caribou mother. Her calf was still too weak to move, and she was ready to defend him with her life if need be.

Ah-Leek turned back and, splashing across the stream again, wandered along the beach to where it ended in a rocky little bluff he could not hope to climb. He was penned in—a determined caribou to the west, five killer whales to the northern beach, and a bank he could not climb to the east and south.

The tide came in, washing along the sides of the stranded killer whales, and the chilly water revived them a little. They began to struggle feebly, and their movements scared the seal pup even more. At a lolloping run he made for the bank and, as the strongest of the stranded killers began to splash even more wildly and to get some movement to its body, Ah-Leek's fears were such that he made a desperate rush at the bank and somehow managed to scramble to the top.

He almost fell back again as he was confronted by the strangest thing: a bird. He had seen sea birds, but had taken no notice of them, but this little bird could not be ignored. It was a red phalarope, and might have been mistaken for a tiny duck.

It was one of the few cock birds which take on the task of hatching the eggs when the hen has finished laying.

The red phalarope cock was frightened. He had never come face to face with a seal pup, and his wings were trembling ready for flight during the ten seconds the two stared at each other. Ah-Leek was no nest robber, nor did he understand that this brave little cock was defending his unborn family. Suddenly the red phalarope gave a little cry, appeared to fall, and then staggered away from the nest with one wing trailing helplessly.

It was an old trick, used against the marauding arctic foxes which appeared on the coast as if by magic as soon as birds began to nest. The phalarope was trying to persuade Ah-Leek that he was disabled, and being unable to fly would be easily caught. If he could decoy this strange creature far enough away from the nest then his eggs might be saved.

Ah-Leek watched, his eyes wide with astonishment; but he did not rush in to grab as the little duck-like bird hoped he would. The phalarope swept into the air and with unbelievable bravery began to fly round and round the young seal's head, so close that a swiftly raised flipper would have brought the phalarope down with a broken neck, back or wing.

Ah-Leek tried to keep his eyes on the flashing little bird, and began to grow dizzy. Exasperated, he barked. Until then he had never barked, only wailed as seal pups do. He barked a second time as the red phalarope swept across his face so close that he could feel the air stirred by the rapid wing beats.

Liking the sound he was making, Ah-Leek barked again and again. Then he waddled forward. His right flipper covered the nest, no more than a hollow in the ground, but the hollow saved the eggs, and they were not even cracked.

The phalarope continued to sweep round the seal pup, its wings moving so quickly they appeared to be a blur around the tiny body. Ah-Leek barked and barked until, tiring of it all, he decided to move on. Happy to call an end to the bloodless battle, the little bird at once withdrew.

Winging away to a tiny pond of melted ice-water, he spun dizzily round and round the edges of the pond. It was not excitement at his victory, but a method of finding a meal. In the vegetation beginning to grow at the water's edge of the pond were thousands and thousands of insects. The whirr of the phalarope's wings disturbed them, and they rose in swarms. It was exactly what the little bird wanted. Insects of this kind were his bread and butter while he was brooding the eggs. He continued his dizzy circling, but now he was taking insects into his beak by the score, feeding fast and furiously while he could.

Five minutes later, almost invisible, he was crouching over the eggs, keeping them warm while the tiny birds within took shape. In another week, if there were no more interruptions, there would be urgent little tappings from the inside of the eggs, and then the chicks would appear.

Within a minute of the phalarope ceasing to torment him with its whirligigging flight about his head, Ah-Leek was enjoying himself. Having discovered that he had a voice he forgot the bird and began to bark. Above the bird-song which filled the air he made himself heard with his rather uncertain

'Wuff-wuff-wuff-wuff'. It was a bit wobbly, but it was a real bark, and Ah-Leek yapped and yapped and yapped. To him the sound was music.

It was music also, but for a different reason, to five men and a boy who were sprawled by the side of a damaged *umiak* no more than a hundred yards down the coast. At first only the boy heard it. Andrew, the young Eskimo who had almost died alongside Ah-Leek, was not so tired as the men.

They had been carrying their damaged boat all day, hoping to come across some place where they could find even the tiniest tree which would provide them with a limb to mend their craft. The walrus bull had done more than slit the bottom of their craft. He had fractured the main keel spar which ran along the bottom.

After rescuing Andrew and giving Ah-Leek his freedom, the hunters had headed for land, but their damaged *umiak* began to fold up. With the keel spar broken they had to throw overboard all the walrus meat, then their tins of petrol, finally even the outboard motor had to be dumped on an ice-floe in an effort to keep their damaged craft afloat. In desperate straits they finally reached land.

They had begun to carry the boat westwards after drying themselves as best they could. They hoped that somewhere along the beach they would find a piece of timber, whether it was driftwood washed in by the tide, or a tree torn from its place on a stream bank.

Their food supply was gone, and they had lived on eggs taken from the thousands of nests which were everywhere on the ground. After a long trek they had lain down to sleep the night before, utterly weary and very hungry. Andrew was the least tired, for he was too young to take much part in carrying the *umiak*, and so he was the one who woke first.

He was achingly hungry. He had tightened his belt the day before, and that had helped him forget the ache, but the hunger was back again now. They had eaten raw eggs, but many of the birds had not yet begun to lay, and it needs a lot of eggs to feed five hungry men and a boy.

Andrew looked at his father and grandfather, then at the three other men. One was his uncle. Their *umiak* lay nearby, the rifles stacked inside it. Throughout the previous day they had kept a sharp look-out for polar bears. Even a bear cub would have provided them with plenty of meat. Mother polar bears ought to be out now with their cubs. After lying up in a den all winter the mother bear would be hungry, and the natural place for them to find food was by the sea; but the Eskimoes had seen no living thing except the birds.

Andrew looked up at the sky. Hundreds of birds were skimming through the air. There were arctic terns, which had spent weeks flying north from the antarctic, though Andrew did not know this. There were tiny buzzing snipe; the larger loons, whose call sounded so lonely in the night; eider ducks, and even one or two cormorants. Inland there were big geese, but they were very wary, and rose in loud-voiced skeins if a man approached anywhere within shooting range. And as yet they had not begun to lay their eggs.

Then, above the myriad bird cries, Andrew heard a sound

which made him stiffen. From the west, and it sounded as if the caller was actually on land, came the barking of a seal. Breathless with sudden excitement, Andrew waited. He did not wonder if his ears were playing tricks on him. He knew they were not. It was a seal! Would it call again?

When Ah-Leek continued to try out his new voice Andrew quietly stepped across and laid a hand on his father's shoulder, then on the shoulder of his grandfather. He did not speak, for the unseen seal was calling and calling. That sound would tell them at once why he had wakened them.

The two men sat up rubbing their eyes at first. Then, as they realized what they were hearing, they hastily got to their feet. Andrew's father wakened his brother and the other two men. At any other time they would have laughed at the idea of five hunters starting out to kill one seal; but there was no laughter in the eyes of the men now.

They were hungry, but that was not the worst thing. With their boat out of action they were crippled. They could walk back to the camp where the women and children would be waiting anxiously; but that would take time. The longer they were without good sustaining food, the less was their chance of surviving.

Each man looked at his gun to make sure it was loaded and the safety catch in the 'off' position. They were all facing in the direction of Ah-Leek, for he had continued to try out his voice.

Andrew's grandfather nodded, and made a motion with his hands; a motion which meant the others must spread out in a line. There must be no mistake. The seal they could hear would provide them with at least two good heartening meals.

'Keep behind'—that was to Andrew when he lined up with the others. Then they spread out, and began to move stealthily in the direction of the unseen seal.

8

Caught between Two Fires

A VAGRANT puff of wind blowing along the coast brought the first warning to Ah-Leek that the strange animals (men) were near. He stopped barking, rose on his flippers and peered ahead. He sniffed again. The scent reminded him vividly of the ice, the walrus, and the two-legged creature which had come out of the sea to join him in his icy prison.

He turned and began to waddle back the way he had come. For the moment he had completely forgotten the five blue-white monsters which lay on the beach. The man-scent was stronger now, and he tried hard to increase his speed. Twice he turned right to the bank which gave access to the beach, but each time he turned back. At each place the bank was six feet high, and the drop to the beach too much for him.

Then, as he passed the phalarope's nest, with the bird winging into the air again in sudden alarm, there was a ringing crack and something struck the half-frozen ground a few yards ahead of Ah-Leek. Without a thought now about the extent of the drop he turned and slithered over the bank, rolling awkwardly on to the sand below.

Behind him he could hear a man calling. It was Andrew's

father shouting to the others, and there was a headlong rush. They had to stop the seal getting into the sea, or it would be lost.

Ah-Leek was confused by his fall, and began a wild dash along the bank, losing valuable seconds before he realized he was not heading towards the water. Turning, he started for the sea, and was within twenty yards of the water before he realized that the five killer whales were still there.

The tide was now almost at full, and two of the monsters were putting up a tremendous struggle for life, rolling and beating the waves with their flippers in an effort to edge back into deeper water. Again there was the sharp biting crack of a rifle, and the bullet threw up a spurt of wet sand no more than a foot ahead of the young seal.

Ah-Leek stopped. Whatever was behind him he did not have the courage to face the killer whales. They looked as fearsome as ever, and even as he stood staring at them the smallest of the five began to slide back into the life-giving sea.

From the top of the little bank came an even more excited yell from the first of the Eskimoes. His eyes had been on the seal first of all, but now he realized there was a far more valuable prize to be had if they were quick.

While Ah-Leek remained motionless on the damp sand, too frightened to move either forwards or backwards, the five Eskimoes jumped down the bank and raced towards the sea. To kill a monster as big as these whales with a rifle was not a thing any of them had ever attempted before.

'Where to shoot?' one of them asked, turning to Andrew's grandfather, and got no more than a dubious shake of the head in reply. A few moments later a second killer whale began to move backwards as the rising tide gave it a little buoyancy. One of the Eskimoes lifted his rifle but, before he could shoot, Andrew's grandfather lifted a hand to wave the barrel aside.

'Do we kill more than we need?' he asked coldly. 'Waste a shot on the whale and the meat will rot. Are there not already three lying dead there? See, their eyes are closed.'

The man lowered his rifle, and all five watched the two surviving killer whales struggle furiously to get back into deeper water. Their tall fins hung slack, sure sign that the whales were weak. Their flippers, which could move them through the water like power-boats, flapped sluggishly.

'They will die,' the man who had lifted his rifle said sulkily. 'Better to kill them now before they drift out to sea and are lost.'

'They will live!' Andrew's grandfather promised, and already it seemed as if the ice-cold water which was now flooding along the parched backs of the two killers was having its effect. It was reviving them, and their struggles grew stronger.

Suddenly Andrew broke the silence. He had come racing down the beach to watch; but he was not pointing at the whales when he yelled excitedly:

'Look, Father, look, it is the same one,' and he pointed to Ah-Leek, who was hugging the sand, afraid to move.

'The same one?' his grandfather queried. 'What do you mean?'

'It is the same seal pup we saw on the ice.' Andrew's eyes were shining with excitement. 'There was a seal on the ice—when I climbed out of the water after the walrus damaged our *umiak*. There was a baby seal fast in the ice, and this is it.'

'How can you tell?' his father asked. 'There are many seal

pups in the water just now. The one we allowed to go free is probably many miles away, and——'

'You are wrong.' It was Andrew's uncle who butted in, and there was a tremor in his usually firm voice as he pointed at Ah-Leek, adding: 'You can see the mark on his head where the bullet creased the fur. Look—the hairs are cut.'

The killer whales were forgotten now, as five men and the boy stared at the frightened Ah-Leek. They were all thinking the same thing. If Ah-Leek had not cried out no one would have known where Andrew was, and the boy would almost certainly have died on the ice. That, they had thought, was good luck.

There was nothing strange about a seal crying; but for the same seal to be here seemed to them more than luck. It had wakened Andrew by barking and now it had led them to this strip of sand, with its prize of three dead killer whales. This was more than good luck, and it made them uneasy.

Though they were visited by missionaries, and had learned about God and Jesus, they found it hard to forget their old beliefs that the world was ruled by good and evil spirits. If hunting was bad, they thought that an evil spirit was punishing them for something they had done wrong.

They believed there were far more evil spirits in their icy world than good spirits, and now they were wondering if this seal pup was a spirit. For them to meet the same creature twice, as they had done, and for it to have helped them each time, was a strange thing.

Andrew's grandfather looked at his companions, and in a husky whisper asked:

'What shall we do? There is something about this seal which frightens me. Why should it help us, when we have already tried to kill it? Why does it not go away? Any ordinary seal would have rushed down to the water; but this one stays here.'

The other men were just as worried. They could understand a good spirit helping them, though it was unusual; but they could not understand the seal pup staying there so quietly, almost as if it was expecting them to do something.

Ah-Leek lay quivering on the damp sand and his eyes were wide with fright. He wanted to get into the sea, but was afraid to move. Between him and the water were the three monstrous killer whales. He did not know that now they could not harm him. In his eyes they were still as terrifying and as dangerous as they had been when they were actually chasing him.

It was Andrew who solved the problem. Tucked into his belt he had a set of fine cords which he used to catch sea birds and duck on the wing. The cords were tied together at one end, but the free ends had small weights on. When swung into the air in front of a flight of duck the cords would wrap about a wing or a neck and bring down a victim for the pot.

Andrew whipped the cords out and at the same moment turned and flung himself down on Ah-Leek. He got a loop about the young seal's flippers in seconds, and Ah-Leek was a prisoner. Before his father could order him to free the seal pup, Andrew said coaxingly:

'Father, he is a luck-bringer. Let us keep him. Let us be kind to him. We can feed him on fish. Then he will see that no ill luck falls on us. He will not let us starve in case he starves.'

His grandfather plucked nervously at the few long hairs which grew on his chin, then nodded. After all, it did seem as if the seal wanted to stay with them, and so Ah-Leek was carried struggling into captivity.

9

Prisoner on the Beach

THEY took their captive to the nearby beach where the damaged *umiak* lay. The old man fastened a cord about Ah-Leek's hind flipper, and pegged him down to the sand. Then two of the men set up a long net a hundred yards out where the tide might bring fish in. With luck the flood tide could bring in some herring, and a good feed of fish ought to keep their captive in better humour. Beyond where the killer whales lay there was the tiny river with its fringe of bushes. From these the men obtained enough timber to repair their damaged *umiak*. They worked quickly but expertly, and made sure the repair was a good and lasting one.

They planned to paddle their craft along the coast to the spot where they had left their wives and children, and the sheet-metal stove on which the food was cooked. There were tents, also, so the *umiak* would be heavily laden on its return trip.

Now that they had such a wonderful prize as three big killer whales, they would need every hand that was free to cut up the great carcasses. The meat would have to be hung out on racks to dry in the wind, and when it was all over they ought to have sufficient meat, and blubber, to keep them happy for the rest of the summer and right through the winter as well.

What had seemed a terrible misfortune when their *umiak* was damaged looked like becoming a great good fortune, and the men firmly believed that the little seal pup was responsible for bringing the good luck.

Because they had been forced to leave their outboard motor on an ice-floe, and would probably never see it again, all five men were going with the *umiak* to ensure as swift a passage as possible. They thought they would be absent for at least two days. Andrew was to stay behind and ensure that the seal pup was kept well fed and happy, and also to make sure that, if any other Eskimo hunters should come along, they could be told to whom the three killer whales belonged.

The young Eskimo was not the least bit worried at the idea of being left alone. His grandfather entrusted him with a rifle and three rounds of ammunition. In any case, the land around would provide him with plenty of food for the two days that he would be alone. He would be able to collect eggs by the dozen, and along the banks of the stream were plants which would provide him with salads—willow leaves and sorrel were to the Eskimoes as lettuce and spinach are to people in more civilized parts of the world.

At this time of the year it was not very difficult to live for a time without meat; and if the men were away longer than expected, Andrew could always cut himself meat from the killer whales. In the cold air the meat would not begin to go bad for some time.

Ah-Leek lay on the beach until the hubbub had died down. He saw the boat go off, and thought he was alone. Then he tried to bite through the thong which held him prisoner. Had the cord been cotton or hemp he might have succeeded, but it was a thong of caribou hide.

His teeth were strong enough to eat fish, but not strong enough to nip through the tough strip of hide. When he finally desisted he lay panting, and it was then that Andrew came to talk to him. The boy had been looking for food. He had collected about twenty eggs, and even managed to catch two early hatched goslings.

From the side of the stream he had gathered fragments of long-dead wood, and when this had dried out a little he proposed to light a fire and cook a meal. In a land where life can be so hard the children are not worried whether eggs are fresh or not. And goslings, which children from more civilized countries might delight in fondling, were no more than a good mouthful of food to a boy like Andrew.

He squatted on his haunches beside Ah-Leek and began to talk to the seal pup. He praised him for his kindness in leading them to the dead whales, and when Ah-Leek simply lay there, watchful, panting, the young Eskimo went on to thank him for saving his life on the ice.

'When the women come', Andrew said earnestly, 'they will all be told how you saved us from hunger. You will be the Great Spirit of our people, and we shall always have good hunting because of you.'

He stretched out a hand, but Ah-Leek gave a short startled

bark and tried to flop away, but his imprisoned hind flipper held him fast. Andrew drew back his hand, looking guiltily behind him. He was glad there were none of the men about to see him. They would have been very angry at the thought that he had tried to make friends with this seal spirit.

Silently he moved away, and began to shave his firewood into fuzz-sticks. Each stick was peeled into shavings so that when Andrew used one of his precious matches the fire would start easily, and burn well. He cooked his eggs and goslings in a pan the men had left him, and added some herbs he had picked.

The tide went out, and Andrew waded almost knee-deep in the water to see if there were any fish with which the seal pup could be fed. The boy did not get wet, for his feet and legs were cased in boots which came almost up to his thigh. They were hand-made by his mother, using sealskin, chewed and chewed until the hide was soft and flexible, and sewn together with caribou sinew. This was a 'thread' which had special advantages. The moment it got wet it swelled up, and filled the holes the needle had made, so that not one drop of water could get through. As a result the wearer could walk into the sea, or into swamps, and so long as the water did not come over the top of his boots he would keep completely dry.

The nets were empty. Not until the tide came in again would there be much hope of a catch, for the fish came in with the tide, and the nets had been staked out as the tide was beginning to recede. By then the fish were swimming back to deeper water.

Andrew told Ah-Leek how sorry he was that there was no food, but promised plenty when morning came.

'The tide will bring in herrings, and perhaps even fingerling salmon. They are very good, and before I eat, you shall have as many as you like,' he said, and nodded soberly to show that he meant every word.

The sun, which had been circling the horizon, dipped out of sight. Somewhere inland, where melted ice had formed a shallow lake over the frozen tundra, a loon called. It was a queer call, almost like a high-pitched laugh, and heard in the night could easily frighten any youngster not born in the wilds as Andrew was.

Head cocked a little, Andrew listened carefully and tried to judge where the loon was. He decided that next morning he would go and find the caller's nest. The loon was a large bird, and its eggs would be large too. Two or three such eggs would make a handsome breakfast, especially with sorrel and willow leaves to add the flavour instead of salt.

Curling up without cover of any kind, Andrew lay for a few moments watching the light to the north. The sky was without a cloud, and the twilight lasted a long time. Up in the north there was a peculiar light which white men called the 'ice-blink'. It was reflected light from the ice-fields, which for the time being had been blown away from the land.

A change of wind could easily blow the ice back again, but Andrew was not worrying about a thing like that. After suffering the great misfortune of a damaged boat, the loss of their outboard motor, and failing to kill a walrus, they had been blessed with three huge killer whales. He dropped off to sleep to dream of tremendous meals of whale meat, and great pieces of whale blubber. Everybody would be very happy when they saw the three carcasses waiting on the beach.

There would be no need for the men to sail out among the ice-pans looking for walrus. They could spend the rest of the short summer curing great masses of whale meat, and catching fish. Their storehouses, inland, would be stocked to bursting, and no matter how bitterly hard the winter was, no matter how fierce the storms were, no one need go hungry.

Ah-Leek was not thinking about the coming winter. He was hungry, but he was making no sound. He was listening. He could hear things too faint for the ears of even an Eskimo boy. He could hear sounds from the distant thicket where the caribou mother had had her calf.

The calf was already strong enough to skip about, but the mother was anxious to keep her baby under cover for at least another day. Then they would join the herd inland. At this time of the year the fierce, cream-coloured arctic wolves came down to the coast, searching for the caribou. A two-day-old baby was not quite strong enough to keep up with a herd going full gallop when chased by a pack of wolves.

Ah-Leek's sensitive ears picked up a score of sounds no human ears could have heard. Somewhere close to the sleeping boy there was the merest whisper of movement from the new grass. It was made by a mother lemming, introducing her babies to the outside world for the first time.

The lemming was so small that a man could have covered it

with his hand. Its fur was warm—brown, long and silky, and the round little body was finished off by a cocky white tail no bigger than a man's finger-nail. The lemming managed to survive the killing cold of the long winter by burrowing into the grasses hidden by a snow bank, and living off the grass roots.

Now, with three tiny babies no bigger than a man's thumb, it came out to look at the brilliant stars which were beginning to show in the darkening sky, looking like tiny chips of ice.

Ah-Leek heard the lemming, though the noise it made was no more than the soft *ssssssh* of grasses being bent aside. In the wide expanse of the sea, with water washing ceaselessly among the mush-ice, Ah-Leek would not have worried about sounds so small. Here, however, he was in a strange world, and he was alone. But for the strange accident which had separated him from the rest of the other baby seals he would have been far to the west, frolicking with them, and safe because of their vast numbers.

He lay awake while the stars brightened, and a thin sliver of moon came out. The tide ebbed to its farthest point, and for a little while there was no sound at all from the sea. Then, as the tide turned and flowed shorewards, wavelets began to break on the sandy beach, adding their strange hiss to the frightening solitude.

Inland, gaunt and hungry, a huge polar bear ambled towards the sea. He had not been lucky in his hunting. Three times he had been just too slow to catch a seal. Twice he had almost got a baby walrus, only to be driven off by the angry father. The bear's skin hung loose as he hunted for food, sniffing the ground, hopefully searching for anything to eat—even such a small thing as a nest with one or two eggs in it.

Then, as a puff of wind blew in from the sea, it seemed as if his luck had changed. He halted, and his head, which looked small by comparison with his huge back, swung snakily from side to side while his wet black nostrils tested the breeze. It was bringing to him several tantalizing scents. There was the smell of seal, a faint man-smell, and another stronger smell of whale meat.

It seemed too good to be true that there should be three sources of food in the area at the same time. Finally deciding from which direction the food scents came, the bear ceased looking for nests and headed for the coast.

To the north-east a brighter light was starting to spread. It was the end of the short night. The sun, which had dipped below the horizon no more than four hours earlier, was rising again to begin a new day. The birds, which had been quiet, began to call and wing their way out towards the sea in search of food. The loon called again, stretching his handsome neck and winnowing his wings as if wanting the world to know how glad he was to be alive.

The old he-bear took no notice. He hardly saw the thin line of gold appear on the distant horizon. He saw nothing of the breathtaking beauty of the ice out to sea as it was lit up by the first yellow rays of the sun. He was old and very hungry.

He reached the stream which gurgled noisily down towards the beach where the three dead killer whales still lay. Once more they were being washed by the advancing tide. He got a faint whiff of caribou but, though he stopped for a moment, sniffing hard, the scent was so weak he decided not to investigate. In the thicket, her heart beating wildly, the mother caribou kept her chin pressed on her baby's back, an urgent signal to him to remain silent.

When the bear passed by on the other side of the stream the mother caribou eased herself and her baby from among the stunted trees and led him at a silent trot towards the higher land. They must join the herd now. Dangers were pressing too close.

On the beach Andrew still slept, though by now the sun was half up and flooding the scene with light. It cast a shadow from Ah-Leek, a long shadow which would grow less and less as the sun rose higher.

On this scene came the polar bear. He could scarcely believe his good luck. The smell of dead whale was very strong to him, and coupled with it was the smell of seal, and the less appetizing smell of a man. The bear's mouth began to water at the scent of seal. They were so easy to kill, and at this time of the year were tender and fat. He needed a good meal, and nothing could be better than a seal.

Ah-Leek did not get the scent of the polar bear at all, for the wind was blowing from the sea to the land. He got only the salt smell and a whiff from a distant herd of walrus. Then, and it made him stiffen in alarm, his finely tuned ears picked up the soft *pad-pad-pad* of the big cushioned paws when the bear was some forty yards away.

Until that moment he had been looking longingly out to sea. A school of whales was out there, and they were disporting themselves noisily. Like the loon which had winnowed its wings, the whales were showing their joy by leaping half out of the water. They hit the surface with a tremendous splash, and in the quietness of the new day the reports were as startling as the ringing cracks of gunshot.

The sea was almost calm, but the antics of the whales were sending ripples to the very beach, so that the tiny waves breaking on the sand were slightly larger and more noisy.

In the midst of these sounds Ah-Leek heard the approach of the bear. He swung round, eyes widening as he tried to catch a glimpse of whatever was drawing near. He could see, but did not recognize, Andrew. The boy was just a shapeless huddle, his knees drawn up, his arms folded across his chest for warmth. So far as Ah-Leek was concerned, Andrew had ceased to exist.

He gave a noisy little gasp as the creamy form of the polar bear came into sight above the high-water bank. The newcomer was sniffing hungrily, but puzzled for the moment by two scents. He could smell the seal well enough, but there was another taint in the air—the man-scent. That was a scent he did not like.

Years before, when he was much younger, and far stronger than now, he had been injured by a long shot from an Eskimo rifle. The bullet had struck him by the ear, and he had dropped senseless. He had regained consciousness to hear a wild, frightening chorus of barks from sled dogs, and standing close by, a skinning knife in his hand, was a strange creature in white—the Eskimo hunter.

The battle which had followed was short and bitter. For the man it was a matter of life or death. He had laid down his rifle; he had been so sure the bear was dead, and had only his skinning knife handy. Had they not struggled to within reach of the howling sled dogs the man would have died.

When the bear turned and fled he was wounded in half a dozen places, while the man was so badly mauled that he had only strength to stagger to his sled. The dogs took him back to his igloo.

From that encounter the polar bear had hated and feared the smell of humans. Whenever spring came and the Eskimoes came down to the coast the bear kept out of their way; but now he was starving, and hunger had driven out fear. He stood on the low bank which separated him from the sand and looked down at the sleeping boy.

His quivering nostrils told him there was a human down there, but his short-sighted eyes had difficulty in picking out the sleeping figure. He stood for a few seconds, teetering uneasily on the edge of the bank; then, as he felt the grassy verge beginning to tremble under his weight, he drew back and moved a few yards to one side where the bank was lower and the slope to the sands more gradual.

Ah-Leek watched him in silence. He had never known how near to death he had been at the paws of a polar bear in the first hour of his life; but there was something about this huge, shaggy-coated creature which frightened him. The young seal was learning to look after himself. Though he was only a few weeks old, fear was beginning to make itself known. He was realizing that there were some creatures to be avoided. Killer whales were one, and this cream-coloured beast was another.

The instinct of almost every wild creature when in danger is to flee—or to 'freeze' and, lying completely motionless, hope the danger will pass. Ah-Leek was lying so still that he might easily have gone unnoticed. His colour blended well enough with the sandy beach, but his unmistakable scent gave him away.

The polar bear walked along the bottom of the low bank to where Andrew was lying. The boy was still huddled in a deep sleep. If he had moved it would have meant almost instant death. A quick blow from a powerful forepaw would have finished him off.

The bear halted with one paw almost on Andrew's thigh. He was ravenously hungry, but there still lurked at the back of his mind the memory of his fight with the Eskimo hunter. That fight had left him out of action for days, and it was weeks before his wounds finally healed. He had never forgotten the man-scent.

Andrew, who had slept soundly, came back to wakefulness to a sniffing sound. Like most people who live by hunting, he wakened as animals waken. One moment he could be sound asleep, and the next he was wide awake. Some sixth sense told him now that he was in danger.

He opened his eyes a fraction, and stiffened at the sight of a polar bear's head no more than two feet from his own face. He could see the dark eyes and the wet black nostrils. The jaws were open a few inches, exposing the cruel fangs. The bear was so hungry that his mouth was watering, and saliva was dripping from the tip of his quivering tongue.

To stay where he was meant death, yet Andrew dare not move. He had never been in such a position before, but he knew that at the first sign of life he gave the bear would bring a heavy paw down on him, as a cat brings a paw down on a mouse.

Andrew was afraid, but Eskimo children grow up with danger at their elbows. They are taught that to die means no more than going into another world, to join uncles and aunts and other relatives. Andrew lay still, looking at the snaky head of the bear through almost closed eyes.

It was then that Ah-Leek made his bid for freedom. The bear had placed one forepaw on the young Eskimo's chest, and was lowering his muzzle to nose at the boy. Then the seal pup tried to get back into the sea.

Seeing the bear preoccupied with Andrew, Ah-Leek turned and hurled himself towards the advancing tide. He had completely forgotten the stout caribou-hide thong fastened securely about one of his rear flippers. As he leaped the thong tightened, and brought him down on to the sand with a thump which shook a half-strangled bark out of him.

At the unexpected sound the polar bear swung round, right paw lifted in case he was about to be attacked. He saw Ah-Leek gather himself and try again to get down to the water's edge, and in an instant Andrew was forgotten. The polar bear had killed and eaten many seals. There was nothing frightening about the smell of a seal. None had ever hurt him; and they were easily killed.

He tore down the stretch of sandy beach, jaws wide, eyes alight in anticipation of a satisfying meal. Ah-Leek barked again in desperation and leaped once more; but again the unbreakable caribou-hide thong brought him down with a breathtaking thump.

There was no escape!

10

The Sea Claims a 'Good Spirit'

AH-LEEK barked twice as the bear rushed at him. No use trying to get to the sea now. Even if the leather thong broke the bear would be on him before he could reach the water. Even if he did get in the shallows the bear was a powerful swimmer, and quite capable of out-swimming a seal pup. There could be no diving or dodging in shallow water.

Some creatures are born with lots of intelligence, and the seal is one of them. Ah-Leek ceased straining at the caribou thong and even waddled towards the bear. Then as the big creamy beast swung a paw which should have killed the seal pup at once, Ah-Leek flung himself to one side. It was a desperate attempt to keep out of the way, but the odds were against him. The bear scooped up half a bucket of sand with his right paw as he missed his aim, then turned and pounced. This time there was no escape; Ah-Leek was at the end of his tether.

The polar bear smashed down with both paws—a thunder-bolt blow which had it gone home would have killed the seal pup immediately. Ah-Leek, however, was still fighting. He tried to rush back the way he had come, and was suddenly imprisoned between the hind legs of the bear. Now he could not move.

Growling impatiently, the bear swung a paw under himself to drag his victim into the open, and as he did so the silence was shattered by a sudden ringing crack. The report sent nesting sea birds winging into the air, wild with alarm.

Crack! Young Andrew fired a second shot, ejecting the first smoking cartridge case with smooth precision. He whipped back the rifle bolt and his second brass cartridge case flipped out, winking in the sunlight.

Andrew had his finger tightening on the trigger for a third shot; but it was not needed. The bear had raised himself to his full height at the first shot, his head swinging half-round on his snaky neck, as if he were wondering whether he really had heard something. Then, a moment after the second shot came, he collapsed without even a grunt. The first shot had killed him instantly. He felt no pain, did not know what had happened; it was a merciful death. He was old, and had spent a long, hungry winter. His hunting powers were waning, and even if he had somehow struggled through the short summer he would almost certainly have been pulled down by wolves when the next winter came. Death by a bullet was a kindly release for him.

Andrew held the smoking rifle to his shoulder for a minute or more after the great cream-coloured beast collapsed. He had often heard the men of the family say that to kill a polar bear with one shot was far from easy. Quite often the big, powerful

beasts went down, only to get up again after a little while as if nothing had happened. They were at their most dangerous then.

The last thin dribble of smoke curled out of his rifle muzzle and was carried away on the light wind. Slowly Andrew lowered the weapon, then dropped the butt between his feet. His hands were beginning to shake a little. Though the morning was crisply cold his forehead was shining with tiny drops of perspiration.

He had gone through an experience which would have frightened the bravest of men, and he was only a ten-year-old boy. To wake and see a polar bear within a foot or so had been a shock which was now beginning to have its effect. His legs began to tremble, and he sat down.

Grabbing the rifle the moment the bear had turned to seek the young seal had been automatic. He had not been thinking of saving the life of Ah-Leek. Up here in a world which was frozen hard for nine months of every year, where life was a constant battle, and food had to be trapped or shot or caught through fishing-holes in the ice, every boy was taught how to use a gun. Every boy was also taught that polar bears were dangerous until they were dead.

When he recovered from the shock he would be proud at the thought that he had killed his first polar bear; for the moment, however, he was too shaken to do anything but sit and tremble.

He came out of his trance with a shock which sent his heart thumping wildly. It seemed as if the bear was not dead after all.

It lay there, but now its fur was lifting a little. It seemed to be breathing again as one flank heaved gently.

Andrew grabbed for the rifle and staggered to his feet. He hurried forward so that he could be sure he would not miss the next shot, and as he did so a round head poked from beneath the creamy flank.

When the polar bear died he dropped on Ah-Leek, almost smothering him. Thin and half-starved though he was, the polar bear was very heavy, and if Ah-Leek had been less courageous than he was he might have died within a few minutes. The thick fur pressed down on him like a blanket, choking off the air so that he was having difficulty in breathing.

The wetness of the sand saved him. When he began to struggle and wriggle the sand became even wetter, as it will when pressed by a hand or a foot. The wetter it became, the softer it became. Ah-Leek, fighting for his life, sank a little lower, and that helped to take some of the crushing load from his back.

Scrabbling feebly with his fore flippers he carved a channel towards the open air, and pushed his round head through the mask of creamy fur just as Andrew lifted his rifle to fire a final shot which would finish off the bear once and for all.

Seal and Eskimo stared at each other. Then Andrew lowered his rifle, only to lift it again and poke the dead bear in the ribs. When that brought no sign of life he laid his weapon on the sand and began deepening the channel Ah-Leek was trying to make.

'I am not going to hurt you,' Andrew said as the seal pup

tried to wriggle back under the bear. 'I want to get you out. The bear is too heavy for me to move. Stay still—if you don't want to die.'

Ah-Leek was hearing a human voice for the second time in his life, and this time, for some reason, it soothed the thumping beat of his little heart. The savage roar of an angry walrus bull he could understand. The rhythmic beat of killer whales' flippers he would never forget. They were things to be feared. This strange sound coming from a creature on two legs ceased to have terror for him.

Relaxing on the wet sand, he waited until Andrew had scooped out a channel deep enough to allow the rescue to be made. Ah-Leek cringed as he felt two warm strong hands take him under the fore flippers. Just for a second his mouth opened, showing his small sharp white teeth. He could have bitten either of Andrew's wrists, but though he turned his head he did not bite.

It needed half a dozen mighty heaves before Ah-Leek was dragged from beneath the bear. The young seal cried out in pain when he was almost freed, for the caribou thong still fastened securely about one of his hind flippers was anchoring him to the peg driven into the sand on the other side of the bear.

A little breathless, Andrew sat and screwed up his eyes in a frown as he tried to drag the prisoner free again. Once more the seal pup wailed at the pain, and then the young Eskimo remembered.

'All right, I am not going to kill you,' Andrew said

soothingly as he drew his bone-handled knife and knelt by Ah-Leek's side. 'I am going to cut the thong. Keep still for a moment.'

He had not meant to set the prisoner completely free, but the moment he had cut the loop pulled tight about Ah-Leek's flipper the seal pup gave a convulsive leap, and began a hoppity-flop down towards the water.

Andrew scrambled to his feet, his eyes suddenly wide with alarm.

'Come back,' he yelled, rushing after Ah-Leek. 'Don't go. There will be lots of fish when I have time to look at the nets. Don't—go——'

Ah-Leek waddled into the tiny waves breaking on the sands, and ducked his head under for sheer joy at the lovely coldness of the water. Andrew splashed into the shallows after him, calling on him not to go away. He chased the seal pup until he was knee-deep.

He stopped then, for the sleek grey-white head of the young seal had dipped below the surface. For a split second there was a ring on the water where the tail flippers had come up as the youngster dived, then he was gone.

When he broke surface again he was a hundred yards out, looking more like a bobbing ball than a young seal. Andrew, a lump in his throat, and an expression of misery on his face, stood and stared. What he would say to his father and grandfather when they returned he could not think. He was sure that the young seal was really one of the few good spirits of the north. It had saved him from the angry walrus; it had led them with its barking to the beach where the killer whales were stranded. Finally, in a moment of the greatest danger of all, it had drawn the polar bear away from him.

Slowly the young Eskimo splashed back through the shallows to the beach. The dead polar bear lay there, a creamy mound on a sand-coloured beach. It was a wonderful prize, and everyone would be proud of him when they came up with the tents and the cooking-stove. He felt as if he had suddenly grown to manhood.

Just for a moment Andrew's face brightened a little, then it clouded once more as he turned and looked out to sea again. He had not wanted to keep the seal pup as a pet. Eskimoes do not have pets. The seal had been much more than that. He had seemed like a guardian angel. Now he was gone. The sea had reclaimed him.

Ah-Leek was so bubbling over with joy when he felt the cold caress of the icy waters that for half an hour he did not even remember that he was very hungry. He dived down to the sea bed, then shot up to the surface again. He stroked his tiny whiskers with his flippers and barked triumphantly.

Finally, as his hunger began to make itself felt, he swam seawards, diving constantly on the look-out for fish. He came on a small school of tom-cod. They were like a platoon of soldiers, all at the same depth below the surface, and all facing the same way.

Their fins were moving placidly, and they were sucking in plankton, those tiny little atoms of life which provide food for even the greatest sea creatures, the whales. It was a wonderfully easy way of life at this time of the year, and the tom-cod were plump.

Yet they must have seen the dark shadow coming towards them, for as Ah-Leek dived the school of tom-cod suddenly scattered. Like specks of dust wafted away by a sudden gust of wind the school broke up.

They were very quick, darting here and there, up and down; but they were not quick enough. Ah-Leek had hunger to drive him on, and at last he caught a plump tom-cod. He shot upwards with the fish in his jaws, and when he broke surface he tossed the fish neatly upwards, caught it by the head, and in a few swift gulps had swallowed his prize. It was the first part of a much-needed meal.

When he had eaten his fill he swam to an ice-pan a mile out to sea. It was one of many scattered over the sunlit waters. Ah-Leek clambered on it and lay basking in the sunshine. He slept in short naps, waking often and raising himself on his fore flippers to make sure no enemy was coming near.

He was young, but he had already learned that, just as he lived off fish, so there were other creatures which lived off seals. In these icy waters the careless died young. Only those who kept eyes and ears open lived to be fully grown.

When he had rested sufficiently Ah-Leek slid quietly into the water again. He did not feel lonely, and was no longer afraid. Yet there was something urging him to swim westwards, and he answered the call throughout the next four days, stopping only occasionally to fish and rest. Then on the fifth day an amazing thing happened.

As he swam towards an ice-pan he realized there was something on it; and there was a new sound in the air. It was a long time in his life since he had heard such a sound—it was the excited, thrilling barking of young seals. What was more, the dark shapes on the ice-floe *were* seal pups.

Like him, they were growing up very quickly. Their fuzzy white baby fur was gone, or almost gone. They had ceased their terrible wailing calls for their mothers. Now they were enjoying life.

Ah-Leek became so excited that he went through the water like a miniature torpedo, his flippers working quickly and smoothly. There were young seals everywhere; the water seemed to boil with them. In addition the ice-floes all had their dark patches, showing where youngsters were basking contentedly in the sunshine.

About a hundred of the more daring had already found their way to the shore and were basking among the rocks, or sliding excitedly about, exploring the new land like children on a picnic.

Why they had come here none of them knew. It was one of the mysteries of life. They had all been deserted by their mothers, just as Ah-Leek had been deserted. They had all cried themselves to sleep for night after night, hoping against hope that the lost mother would return.

Then, as if some mysterious signal had been given, they had come together in groups. Small groups had joined other groups, until they had become a mighty herd of young seals.

Like the others, Ah-Leek was not worrying about the

reason why he had swum westwards alone. Something had made him follow the same track through the sea that countless thousands of young seals had taken through countless years. He was happier now than he had been since the day his mother had deserted him.

Scrambling on to an ice-floe, he stuck his nose against another seal and both twitched their whiskers in delight. Every young seal seemed ready to play, and ready to welcome any other seal. Ah-Leek barked and barked, adding his voice to the song of joy which was filling the air.

After half an hour's rest on the wet ice of a small floe he slipped into the sea and joined a group of seal pups who were making the water white with the foam they were kicking up. They played like children who have just come out of school.

In a few brief weeks the summer would be over. The days would grow very short, and savage winds from the North Pole would bring back the ice. It would swing the floes towards the land. Ice-stars would appear on the water and in the darkening nights the northern lights would flame like pink, green and electric-blue fire across the sky. They were the heralds of the storms which began the winter.

By that time the seals would have swum away. No one would tell them to go. None of them would know why they went; but they would swim away. Then, when winter locked the seas with thick ice, they would be scattered, each one with its own breathing-holes in the ice.

They would all be stronger, wiser and more able to take care of themselves. For the time being, however, Ah-Leek was one of a multitude of happy children. This was the playground of the children of the ice, and though he was almost a week late in arriving there was no one to punish him for not being on time.

Barking his joy he plunged into the midst of a group, and the play went on until suddenly one dived below and came up with a fingerling salmon. That was a signal for all to dive and look for food. It was lunch time for the seal pups!

About the Author

ARTHUR CATHERALL was born in England and since 1935 has written more than sixty books for both children and adults. Mr. Catherall has traveled all over the world, has walked across Northern Lapland carrying food packs on his back, and has worked aboard herring drifters and trawlers in the Atlantic and off the shores of Iceland. *Lone Seal Pup* is based largely on his intimate knowledge of the Arctic. When not writing, Mr. Catherall is an enthusiastic camper, hiker, and mountain climber. He is married and the father of two grown children.

About the Artist

JOHN KAUFMANN has been drawing all his life and illustrated his first children's book in 1961. A native New Yorker, Mr. Kaufmann lives on Long Island with his wife and two children. One of his chief interests is bird-watching and he is a frequent visitor to nearby beaches where he paints watercolors of shore birds and seascapes.